RACING CHAOS

RACING CHAOS

The Adventures of Captain Cassy
Book 1

By
Emma Montgomery

Blue Canary Publishing LLC
Portland, Oregon

Copyright © 2022 by Emma Montgomery
Blue Canary Publishing LLC

Paperback ISBN: 979-8-9864717-2-3
                979-8-9864717-0-9
E-Book ISBN: 979-8-9864717-1-6

Cover designs by vincenzoingenito_tattooer
Katarina Naskovski/nskvsky
and Emma Montgomery

Printed in the United States of America

To my family
who have always supported my dreams

CONTENTS

Floating naked in space is not how you would imagine it. Your blood does not boil; your body does not instantly turn to ice. Your eyes do not pop out of your head. You simply are. Suspended in the vacuum, you just exist.

Tef found it oddly freeing, looking out onto the dazzling light show of the universe. A nebula, purple and orange with towering, swirling plumes, floated gently to his right. To his left, a binary star danced. He could almost imagine he was alone out here, relaxing with a front row seat to the universe.

But of course, he wasn't alone. Behind him, somewhere, was the airlock that doubled as his execution chamber. Was it really only seconds ago he was inside, fighting in vain to reach his murderer? The Chaos, with its hulking, inhuman mass, must be hovering just behind him, although he could hear no sound in the vacuum.

Did I succeed? he wondered, vaguely, his thoughts spreading like the tendrils of the nebula. Is their blood on my hands? Black spots crowded his vision. His brain was shutting down. If only he could talk to someone. His vast knowledge, knowledge that held the lives of thousands of innocents, was fading to nothingness as his cells died. The black spots were everywhere, an invasion of oblivion he couldn't fight. He forced his eyes to focus on the fiery majesty of the nebula, holding the light in his eyes for as long as he could. It wasn't long.

Behind him, Chaos waited. It hovered silently behind the tiny body, a whale contemplating a krill. Two small panels opened on the front of the bulbous ship, revealing two gun barrels. They jerked to life, locking their sights on the body that had so recently been Tef.

The guns fired.

Chaos took no chances.

There was a good view of Res4 from the roof of the communications tower. Of course, just because a view is good doesn't mean there is anything to look at. Res4 sprawled before me, a collection of low, ugly metal roofs, glittering dully against an endless backdrop of desert.

I dangled my legs over the side of the tower, shading my eyes with dirty fingers as I scanned the maze of corrugated metal and dirt paths that converged below me to form the main hub of the settlement.

My eyes wandered to the scrap pile. Twisted rebar, cracked pots, rusty power converters, frayed wires, used batteries, worn out shoes: you name it, the heap had it. Some people complained that it was an eyesore. To me, it was a treasure trove.

I loved scouting for scrap. It was a thousand times better than working in the mine. And from my special perch, I could see parts of the heap not visible from the ground. I pulled out my binoculars. Most of the junk was, well, junk, but after several minutes of searching I found what I was looking for.

I slid down one of the tower's support poles, earning gasps from the people standing nearby as I hit the ground. I gave them a smile and a wave, but honestly, if they weren't used to me doing that by now, they were never going to learn.

They wouldn't get the chance.

Big Bihn was sitting on the remains of his tractor as I walked up to the heap. He squinted at me through watery eyes, his pipe dangling between yellow teeth. "That you, Cassy girl? Happy graduation tomorrow!" he wheezed.

"Thanks, Bihn," I said, stopping next to the ragged wheel of his tractor and peering up at him, my dirty hand shielding my eyes from the glare of the setting sun. "How's the trade?"

Bihn grunted and scratched himself through dirty overalls. "Could be worse. Fancy tradin' ship parked for a few hours an' bought some ore from the Company. Then Weevil raiders lugged in some rusted scrap from the desert an' got mad I wouldn't pay solid buks for it. Traded some junk just to get 'em to beat it." Bihn spat in the dirt, then looked down at me with a twinkle in his eyes. "Joren isn't here though, if that's who you're looking for. I think he's out with Mae and Drak. Shouldn't you be with 'em?"

Like me, Joren had a side hustle in scrapping. He was the only other mining trainee who spent as much time scrapping as I did. I even had a sneaking suspicion that Bihn was training Joren to replace him as scrap overseer. It wasn't an official position, but the mine management on Res4 was smart enough to know the scrap heap needed some oversight, so Bihn took bribes for better access and the Company turned a blind eye. It was one of the better gigs on Res4, to be honest. Ever since I could remember people told me that Bihn would be killed by raiders any day now, it was inevitable, but most of those people were dead in the mine and Bihn was still sitting on his tractor.

"I'm not here for Joren, I'm here to salvage," I said, digging in my pocket for the requisite bribe, a mostly uneaten mock-choc protein bar. "Can I buy five minutes in the heap?"

Bihn sat up, a dirty overall strap sliding off his blistered shoulder. "What do you 'spect to find in five minutes? You sure you don't want a full half-hour? I'll give you a discount."

"Nope," I said, handing him the payment. "Five minutes is all I need."

I found what I was looking for in about 40 seconds, heading directly to the pile I had identified from the tower. On top of a mound of industrial trash was an old solar speeder, rusted and inoperable. The junk metal was blistering hot in the light of the setting sun, but I was still wearing my sturdy mining coveralls and gloves from my last shift. Stradling the busted scooter, I pulled the hairpin out of my bun, letting my hair fall around my shoulders as I inserted the flat end into the top of the screw. A few twists and the screw was free. The item went into my backpack, my hair went back up in a twist, and I started down the pile.

Bihn gave me a wave as I left. Joren, Mae, and Drak were still nowhere to be found.

As I passed through the dusky center square, their location became obvious. Lights and laughter poured from a squat, rusty building, and I could hear the faint sound of dance music playing over crackling speakers.

Oh, right.

There was a party tonight. My cohort would all be there, celebrating tomorrow's graduation. I almost never went to Tim's tavern, which had given me the reputation of a clean-living homebody who never did anything but mine, scrap, and sleep. It didn't make me very popular, but that was fine with me. Being popular on Res4 was not one of my priorities.

I wouldn't exactly call myself a homebody though.

"Hey, Cassy!"

Mae was standing in the doorway, her fiery hair backlit and glowing. It was coiled on top of her head and pinned like mine, but somehow she managed to make the simple style look fashionable. She made everything look good. Even her orange mining coveralls were rolled up at the cuffs and belted tight around her waist, making her look more like the heroine in an action holo than a poor mining apprentice.

I looked down at myself, suddenly self-conscious. I always looked the same. Brown hair, tan skin, dirty and rumpled clothes. The only thing interesting about me were my amber eyes, but amber was just another shade of brown. Whatever. It didn't matter.

"Where are you going?" Mae called, waving me over. "You weren't planning to skip the party, were you? Get over here!"

Reluctantly, I slunk over. "I'll come back later, okay?" I lied. "I have some stuff I want to do first."

Mae rolled her eyes. "Stuff to do? It's our graduation party! Nothing is more important than this."

Grabbing my hand, she pulled me into the tavern.

Inside, it was packed. Not that it took many people to fill the small room, which consisted of a short bar, a few metal stools, a corner-mounted radio speaker, and one large armchair pulled up to a fireplace that someone had drawn on the wall in chalk. Teenagers stumbled around, clinking metal cups full of Tim's brew of the week and laughing. Drak was standing on a stool doing some kind of dance while a few of the girls jokingly cheered and pretended to throw him money.

"Cassy!"

I turned to the bar. Joren was waving at me, his cheerful green eyes almost startling against his dark face. I smiled back. Joren was my other best friend. We were inseparable as kids, but as we got older, I started spending more time with Mae. Then I began my side project and stopped hanging out with anyone at all.

I shuffled my feet and turned to leave, but Mae grabbed me. "Don't go!" she cried, throwing her arms around my neck and pulling me into a tight hug. She smelled like wine and soap. I probably smelled like dirt and sweat. I pulled away. "I have something to do, okay? But we'll talk tomorrow morning. I'll tell you everything then."

Mae gave me a teasing look. "You're always so mysterious! Oh well, I love you anyway."

Standing on her tiptoes, she gave me a kiss on the cheek. "Try to make the end of the party, okay? I know Joren wants to see you." She winked.

"We'll see," I fibbed. I felt bad lying to her, but after all, it was just for one more night.

A noise from the far side of the room caught my attention. Drak, who had just taken a huff of engine cleaner, was challenging the room to an arm-wrestling competition. Mae laughed and clapped, moving closer to the entertainment.

Slowly, I backed out of the bar.

This time, no one noticed. Once outside I turned and headed west, away from the lights and noise.

The streets were a narrow maze once you left the CenterRes, but I knew them like the back of my hand. Small storefronts quickly turned into even smaller houses, two or three rooms at most. The first houses I passed were modest but well made, with painted porches and glass windows, but the closer you got to the outskirts the more run-down the buildings became. Glass windows turned into plastic windows, then no windows at all. From an open door I could hear someone singing an old Earth lullaby.

I kicked a rock, watching it roll down the unpaved road and into the gutter.

My house was at the farthest end of the main road, a small plot assigned to me when I turned twelve and took the option to move out of the kid's hall. At least, that's how old the Company had said I was. I had been dropped at Res4 as an infant, with no explanation or identification. There was a lucrative trade in babies in this sector, and slavery was a bigger business every day. Some babies were worth a lot of money. But the Company got me for free. I had no value, so they told me.

My house was small, just one room with a pit in the corner, but it was clean and I had saved enough money for a bedroll, a table, a lamp, and a promotional poster for Imago 5, a nearby resort planet. Sometimes travelers would stop here on Aavikko to get kakorine ore on the cheap and browse the scrap. They would bring colorful souvenirs and trade them for enormous profit to rural idiots like myself. I traded a whole bag of top-quality engine washers for that poster, which was outright robbery, but totally worth it. I loved that poster. It showed a pink waterfall splashing into a lagoon, with a beautiful woman stepping from the frothing water as a neatly uniformed waiter offered her a sparkling drink. She was giving the viewer a cheeky wink. I liked to pretend I was that woman, happy and safe with nothing to do but indulge myself. I would climb to the top of the waterfall and survey that world, imagining what else lay beyond the borders of the flimsy paper. Sometimes I would find an enormous glittering ocean teaming with life. Other times I would find a resort with food and music and dancing. When I was very tired, usually after a triple shift, I would pretend the whole world was that one lagoon, and I would send away the waiter and float alone in the gentle pink foam.

My most prized possession, however, was my holo of Captain Ace, Volume 1. It was under my bed. I didn't have a way to play it but I liked having it all the same. Sometimes holos would make their way to Res4 and the Company would run them in the mess hall. After this one had been played several times I asked to keep it and they said sure. It was a good season too, with Ace winning the Diomedes 100 in the season finale. Mae had been jealous, so I gave her the box with the episode list and an illustration of Ace, splay-kneed in his captain's chair. She had a big crush on Captain Ace, or at least Perk Hamlin, the actor who played him in the holos. The flattened box hung above her bed. The thought made me smile. We always imagined heading off into the galaxy like Captain Ace, together on our own crazy adventure.

I crossed the small room and pushed through the loose panel at the back, stepping clandestinely into the craggy expanse of desert beyond. There was a ridge of rock directly behind my house that gave a border to the back of the settlement, providing a visual barrier from the desert to the west.

Which meant that from CenterRes, no one could see me leave.

The western desert was a seemingly endless wasteland of jutting cliffs and coarse sand, punctuated by garbage heaps, raider camps, and the occasional wrecked ship. The area received a disproportionate number of crashes due to the unstable Proteus nebula, which loomed like a purple guardian in the sky. Members of the Company were heavily discouraged from entering the desert, and there wasn't much of a point. If you worked in the mine full-time you would never have the time to find a wreck, salvage it, and make it back between shifts. Maybe if you had a working solar speeder, but there hadn't been one of those in Res4 since Crazy Ramon lost his mind two years ago, stole the Company's last speeder, and was never seen again. So, scrappers relied on the informal network of raiders, professional scavengers, and itinerant merchants to move the scrap into Res4 where the best was sold, repaired, and resold to travelers. Having the scrap heap gave us a slight edge over the other Res sites in terms of attracting travelers for direct ore sales. Res1 might be nicer, but if you came down to Res4 you could get your ore *and* whatever parts your ship needed, as long as you didn't mind things second-hand.

It was a pretty good system, all things considered.

The sun was setting but there was still enough light from the nebula to make my way down the familiar path.

The desert glowed red in the sunset, irregular stripes of mineral deposits painting the landscape with strokes of purple and yellow. I followed the path for a half mile until it curved around a huge stone formation, sticking out of the desert like a giant thumb. Grinning with anticipation, I turned the corner.

And there she was, a glorious silhouette against the brilliant red sky.

A ship.
MY ship.

Chapter 2
Graduation Day

The *Erebus* was a four-by-nine-meter tube sitting lightly on three landing struts. In the twilight she looked solid black, but that was far from the case. Most of her parts were from Gilian Small Transporters, or GSTs, but from so many different models and trims that almost nothing matched. Many of the interior parts were from completely different types of vessels, ranging from solar scooters, like the salvage from today, to a ridiculously overpowered XKPR-9 engine that was probably from a drug-runner's transport, according to Big Bihn. It wouldn't have a fancy jump drive, but here in Sector 3 you rarely saw jump drives outside of racing events, so that didn't matter. It would get me around.

The name *Erebus* came from a holo about black hole exploration. The holo itself was terrible, to the point where people said a slaver ship tossed it into a deal for free because even the slaves were sick of it. I didn't remember a lot of it, but at one point the eccentric head scientist pointed at the viewscreen and exclaimed dramatically, "Forward men! If we fall, we fall as explorers, as men of the *Erebus* and *Terror*!" The phrase had lodged in my mind. "Men of the *Erebus* and *Terror*." It ran through my head as I pushed carts and moved rocks and fixed scrap in the dead of the night. I didn't really know what it meant, but it sounded powerful. *Erebus* and *Terror*. *Erebus* and *Terror*. Naming my hodgepodge ship *Terror* seemed a bit dramatic, but *Erebus*...I liked it. It had an old fashioned, solid sound to it, like it came from Earth. It probably had.

I hit a button on the stern of the ship and a section of the hull folded down, revealing four steep stairs leading to the door of an airlock. I climbed in. After the glow of the desert, my eyes took a moment to adjust to the dim interior. Beyond the airlock was a short hallway covered in sliding panels that concealed storage compartments. A taller panel, otherwise identical to the rest, led to a practical, all-in-one bathroom with a shower spigot dangling optimistically from the ceiling. Below me was a trapdoor to the engine crawlspace. The room doubled as the sleeping quarters, with two beds slotted broadside in opposite walls. Beds might be an exaggeration — they were six-by-two-foot shelves covered with thin blankets. This wasn't exactly luxury travel.

A ladder on the far wall led up to the next level, a stark, windowless box about the size of the mining elevator. I climbed in. This was going to be my kitchen and common room, although right now it just contained bagged supplies, making it look more like a storage closet than the main room of a spaceship. In the ceiling, a round opening led to the cockpit, connected by a second ladder. I crawled inside and grinned. Proudly displayed in the center of the space was a captain's chair; a proper, padded, blue wingback swivel chair with armrests. It was the crown jewel of my salvage efforts, next to the XKPR-9 engine. It made the cockpit look almost professionally built. Almost.

The chair was facing a panel of controls and a viewscreen, currently blank.

I slid into the chair, relishing the feel of the smooth cloth under my palms. *This is it,* I thought to myself. *This is my last night on Aavikko.*

On the left armrest was another, smaller control panel. A switch was missing, revealing the short nub of a screw. Twisted around the screw was a rusty inch of wire. I had been using that wire as a make-shift switch for months, ever since I found the chair. The panel was mostly broken but that circuit worked, and I had hooked it up to control the viewscreen. I'd been worried that a switch wouldn't come my way before graduation and *Erebus* would have to launch with a janky captain's chair, but my last-minute dive in the heap had proved fruitful. Out of my pocket I produced the piece from the speeder. My final piece of salvage.

It was just a plain little black switch, but it screwed on perfectly, and when I flipped it, the lights snapped on with a satisfying *click.* The viewscreen blinked into attention, showing the empty expanse of the desert before me. There was nothing left to do. The *Erebus* was ready.

The next morning took an eternity to arrive. Instead of sleeping, I ran system check after system check, accidentally falling asleep in my chair just before dawn. I woke with a start and a neck cramp several hours later, panicking that I had missed my shift.

Then I remembered what day it was.

I grinned.

I would never have to worry about missing a shift again.

My cohort had the day off as a reward for graduating, which simply meant that we had repaid the company for supporting us during our decade of 'training.' Now, we would finally start pulling a salary, albeit a small one. The duties were essentially unchanged. I'd been doing an adult load since I hit puberty.

I needed to find Mae. The time for secrets was over.

If you had told me when I started building *Erebus* that I could hide it from Mae all these years, I would have told you to kick rocks. Impossible. But it happened without even trying. I suppose, at first, I was a little embarrassed. It was embarrassing to think I could build a ship. Sure, there were plenty of ship parts and we were mining a power source, but it's not what people *did* on Aavikko. The Company wouldn't like it, for one, and if you pissed off the Company you burnt most of your bridges, planet-side. But my thinking was, if the ship worked, who cared what the Company thought? It seemed worth it to try, and besides, what else was I doing with my evenings? Parties at Tim's had zero chance in getting me off planet, no matter how much I drank or how many people I snogged.

And I did want to get off-planet. Desperately. It's not like anything was particularly wrong, I knew others had it worse, but I had this image lurking in the back of my mind of graduating and my whole life being laid out before me. I was supposed to be a good little trainee because, why? So I could graduate and join the Company, take an assigned identity like it had anything to do with me, hit the benchmarks needed to get promoted, then slowly decline until I took the long walk into the desert?

And that was the best-case scenario. That the company used me gently enough that I was *allowed* to grow old.

Pass.

The dream really began when I found a manual for a standard GST, complete with diagrams and explanations of how the different pieces worked together. The manual was made specially for owners to make repairs with limited resources.

It was like finding the Holy Grail.

Deciding to build my own ship was a pretty easy choice after that. And I didn't actually need to *build* a ship, not really, I just needed to find and repair several partial ships and weld them all together. The riskiest thing I did was occasionally borrow the anti-gravity pads from maintenance to lift the heavy pieces. Even that wasn't much of a risk. I was friendly with storage staff and could always figure out some excuse.

Despite my furtiveness, what I was doing wasn't strictly *illegal*. It wasn't even against Company regulations. I'd checked. Flipping scrap was allowed as long as it was on your own time. Encouraged, even, as it fueled the trade that attracted direct buyers to Res4 over the other Res sites. And there was nothing in the rules preventing a person from building things from scrap, even building transportation. *Using* that transportation was where the rules got tricky. Trainees technically had no travel restrictions, but if you missed a shift the Company would fine or imprison you. Fining was often worse than imprisonment, because it put you further into debt, and as long as you had Company debt, they owned you. Once you were a full Company member you needed special permission to leave your Res, and no boss was going to approve your leave unless it benefited the Company. But yesterday fulfilled the last day of my training contract, and the signing ceremony for my new contract was at the graduation party this afternoon.

At this moment, I was technically a free woman.

Despite it being only nine in the morning, the door was open at Tim's.

I found Joren cleaning cups with a cleanish rag. "Hey!" I called as I entered. "Whatcha doing?"

Joren started in surprise, almost dropping the cup. Recovering it deftly, he gave me a smile, his cat-green eyes lighting with interest.

"Well," he said, "we pulled an all-nighter, so when I woke up *on* the bar, I thought the least I could do was help clean." He put down the cup and picked up another. "Where did you disappear to?"

I walked over to the bar and grabbed a cloth to help, ignoring the question. "Looks like you guys had a good time. Where's everyone else?"

He nodded to the far corner. The back of a curly dark head was peaking over the top of the tavern's armchair. Drak was still asleep, or unconscious, with an empty cup dangling in one hand.

"I think everyone else got themselves home. Where did *you* go?" he asked again.

I shrugged, walking over to Drak and delicately extracting the cup. He gave a snore and wiggled but didn't wake up. "I was fixing up some scrap," I said, truthfully. "You know how it is."

"Yeah, sure," Joren said slowly. For some reason his look made me uncomfortable, like he was seeing right through me. I focused on cleaning the cup.

"Cass," he said in the same slow voice. "What's going on with you?"

I shrugged. He continued to watch me.

"Cass...I know something is up. What is it?"

Finishing with the cup, I walked over and set it on the bar in front of him. Then I looked him squarely in the face.

"Are you signing on with the Company?" I asked.

Now it was Joren's turn to clam up, crossing his arms across his broad chest. We stared at each other.

"Hey you guys!" sang a bright voice from the doorway. We both jumped. Mae waved and walked towards us, spotless in a blue floral dress that matched her eyes, curly red hair unbound and bouncing around her dimpled face. "Is Drak still asleep? And there you are, Cassy! You sneak, you missed the whole party! And you are still so dirty!"

I looked down at myself. I had gone straight from the mine to the heap, to working on the *Erebus*, to sleeping in my clothes. I was filthy. I probably should have washed and changed before coming here.

Mae shook her head at me. "You can't possibly walk around on graduation day like this. You look like a sand rat! Where is that green dress of yours?" She looked pityingly at Joren, as if apologizing for my appearance.

Joren laughed, "She looks fine. She looks like Cass."

I rolled my eyes, "That dress is awful. I've had it forever, it's falling apart, and it makes me look like a little kid."

"You look very pretty in it. But if you don't like it, why didn't you get a new one? This is a big day! Didn't you plan at all?" She brushed a smudge of dirt off my cheek, then smiled at me with exasperation.

I smiled back, "Well, we can't all be as smart as you. I'll shower and change later. Right now, I have something to show you, remember?"

Joren cleared his throat, "I should get back to Bihn. I said I would help him out this morning."

I hesitated. A part of me wanted to say something, to invite him along.

But I had only budgeted supplies for two. And what would Big Bihn do without Joren?

Making the decision for me, Joren gave us a parting wave and ducked out the back. I caught a glimpse of the heap beyond as the door swung shut.

Mae was looking between us with a smug look on her face. Rolling my eyes again, I gestured for her to follow and headed out the front door.

We walked along the dusty path to the outskirts of the Res, Mae chatting happily about the upcoming graduation ceremony, about how we would get to turn in our rusty orange training coveralls for an official blue set, and how much better that would look with her hair. "Drak and Joren are probably going to stay assigned to the deep work, but we might get reassigned! You might be put on maintenance since you are better with machines than people." She grinned cheekily. "And I'll be assigned to corporate sales. Could you even imagine? My job will be talking to travelers!"

"Grads from Res4 never get assigned to sales," I reminded her. "It's always transfers from Res1 or 2." I yanked a leaf off a scrubby silverleaf bush and popped it in my mouth, enjoying the brief kick of dopamine it provided. "But are you sure Joren is going to sign on?"

Mae shot me a confused look. "Of course. What else would he do? He's trained for ten years to join the Company. He's not going to throw that away." She grinned and gave me a friendly nudge, "He's really good at his job, you know. I think he could make head getter, and soon! Wouldn't that be fantastic?"

Fantastic is not the word I would use. "It's really dangerous," I said.

Mae shrugged, "It's not as dangerous as other jobs. It has prestige, plus the pay is much higher."

"So? What's there to buy?"

She shot me a look. "You just like complaining. This is a happy day and you can't spoil it. Anyway, aren't you going to show me something cool? We've been hiking through the desert for *ages*."

I grinned, instantly forgetting about Joren and the Company. "It's right around this rock. Close your eyes."

Mae groaned, "Really?"

I laughed, suddenly nervous. "Yes. It's a surprise."

She sighed but obediently closed her eyes, holding out a hand for me. Taking it, I gently guided her around the boulder.

My ship rounded into view, glowing in the diffuse morning light. I stopped, took a deep breath, gave the *Erebus* a nod, and said proudly, "Open your eyes."

Mae opened them. "Whoa!" she said, sounding startled. She took a step back and let go of my hand.

I grinned at the *Erebus* and waited for Mae to continue her praise.

Silence.

I waited another beat.

Nothing.

Turning around, I saw her staring at the *Erebus* with eyebrows raised, looking confused. After a moment she said slowly, "So, what am I looking at?"

"It's my ship!" I said, throwing my arms open in a "ta-da" and giving her my biggest smile.

Mae looked past me, concern written across her face, "Okay..." She scanned the desert nervously. "How did it get here? Because if it belongs to raiders we shouldn't be hanging around. Cassy, we should tell the Company."

"Calm down," I said. My grin was so wide I could feel it cracking the dust on my face. "It has nothing to do with raiders. This is MY ship."

Mae relaxed slightly. "Then...okay...." She turned and gave me a hesitant smile, seeming to realize I was expecting a positive reaction. "It looks like a good find! I don't know much about salvage but it's...it's got a lot of parts, so that's probably good. Maybe it can even fly. We can tell Bihn about it on the way back to Tim's." She gave me a pat on the back.

"Mae," I said, shrugging off the pat. "This is my ship. I built her. Her name is *Erebus*. And she doesn't just fly. She's space worthy."

"Air-Bus?"

I blinked. "No, *Erebus*."

"And what do you mean, you built it?" Mae said as though she hadn't heard me. "It does *not* look safe."

"She's safe!" I said, indignantly. "At least, she should be. I haven't tested flight yet. I was wondering if you wanted to take her for a spin? She's built for two."

She looked at me as if I just sprouted another head. "What? Are you crazy?"

"You need to see inside!" I ran over to the control panel and activated the stairs. They folded down, softly hitting the dirt at my feet.

Mae jumped back. "Cassy, stop! Slow down and tell me what you are doing."

I was buzzing with adrenaline. I wanted to grab her and drag her into the cockpit, the common room, the bunks, but she was still backing away with a troubled look on her face, her eyes darting between me and the ship.

"You know how we've always talked about flying out of here?" I said, my words tripping over each other with excitement.

"Yes...?" she said, cautiously.

"Well, I'm going to. Today. And I want you to come with me."

"What? Today?" She stopped in her tracks, blue eyes huge. "You can't possibly be serious."

"Of course I'm serious. Come, look inside!" I reached for her hand, but she pulled it away.

"Cassy, you're scaring me. You can't honestly think you can do this."

I dropped my arm, smile wavering. "Of...of course I can. Or, at least I can try. I've been holding off on flying her until my trainee contract was up because, well, you know the Company, but I've been running tests for months and everything looks really good."

"But...you work tomorrow..."

I shook my head, "No, I don't. Don't you understand? You know I've never wanted to sign on, so here's my solution. For both of us."

Her eyes went even wider, "You aren't joining the Company? You *actually* aren't joining?" Her voice raised in pitch. "Cassy, I know we like to complain about work, but you've been training for this your whole life! You *have* to sign on!"

I stared at her. "What?"

"You can't seriously want to throw away your livelihood, your home, *everything*, to go off in this tin can?" She gave me a scrutinizing look. "Is this cold-feet about graduating and becoming an adult?"

"No..." I said slowly, confused. "It's pretty much the opposite of cold feet. I don't want to live here, so I'm not going to. And I know *you* don't want to live here either. We've talked about it a thousand times. There's nothing for us here."

There was a long pause. Then Mae sighed, "Cassy, this isn't how I wanted to tell you..."

"What?"

"Drak asked me to marry him last night." She gave a small smile. "I said yes."

I felt my heart twist in my chest. What? Marry? *Marry Drak?* I hadn't realized they were serious, or even in a proper relationship. When had this happened? The only guy Mae ever talked about was Perk Hamlin. "We can bring Drak." I said quickly, panicking.

She shook her head. "He can't leave. He's racked up a bar tab with Tim. The Company is going to buy his debt, but he still has to work it off."

She took a deep breath and said in a voice of forced calm, like she was talking to a child, "So you see, we can't go on some crazy adventure right now. This is real life, Cassy."

I felt like I was going insane. "So...you are going to stay here, sign your life over to the Company, never leave Aavikko, which probably means dying in the mine, all in order to bunk with what, one of the ten guys you've ever met?" I looked at her in confused disbelief. "Do you even love him?"

Mae exploded, "STOP BEING SO NAIVE! Love? Spaceships? Who do you think you are? If you had a brain in that silly head of yours you would face reality and take what is being offered. You need to seriously adjust your expectations, you...you ungrateful..." her voice broke. "You are supposed to marry Joren, don't you know that? Everyone else does. My god, have you even thought of *him*? How could you be so selfish!"

Everything was upside down. "I'm selfish? *Me?*" I threw up my hands, completely bewildered, hot tears welling behind my eyes. "You've apparently planned my entire life for me. *I'm selfish?*"

She crossed her arms and looked at my ship, clearly unimpressed. "I've always defended you, you know. When people said you lived in a fantasy world. That you thought you were too good for us. That you were a fool. I always defended you. But they were right."

Her words stung like a slap.

"The Company won't take you back, not Res4 at least. And you've never been to Res5 or Res6," Mae continued, firmly. "It's not like this at all. We are lucky. Do you really think other places are like the holos? Even if places like that do exist, they are systems away, and for other people, and that...that ship...you can't be serious."

I took a ragged breath and tried to get myself under control. When had I started crying? This was all going so wrong. I had to try again. "Mae, please, listen to me. It's a real ship. It flies. I worked really hard." I tried to meet her eyes but she looked away. I took another breath. "You're right, I'm not Captain Ace. But I am Captain Cassy." Despite everything, that made me smile. "I'm Captain Cassy, and I'm offering you a chance to leave. You don't have to take it now. It's an open invitation. And you can leave and come back if you want. But I am leaving. Today."

She turned to look at me. Her face had hardened into an expression I didn't recognize.

"Why didn't you tell me you were doing this?" she asked finally.

"It was a surprise," I replied, lamely.

"You realize you are basically a child, right?"

I sighed, suddenly very tired. "So are you. Have fun at your wedding."

Mae turned her back and walked away.

Chapter 3
New Plan

I sat on the steps of the *Erebus*, face streaked with dried tears. I had caught a glimpse of myself and it wasn't pretty, but my face was the least of my problems. I ran home as soon as I was sure I wouldn't bump into Mae, knowing I had to clear out fast. It only took a minute to shove my remaining belongings in a canvas sack and hurry back. I left the Captain Ace holo and the travel poster for Mae. She could have those. I was going to see the universe for myself. On the floor beneath the poster I sat a small communications device and scribbled her name. It was synced to my receiver on the *Erebus* and could send quantum communications that were impossible to block, track, or intercept. I had bought it to use to communicate with Mae if one of us left the ship, and I didn't see a reason to change that plan.

Why hadn't I told her about my ship earlier? Was it because I was afraid this would happen?

I knew there was a possibility she wouldn't want come with me, but in my wildest dreams I hadn't expected a reaction like *that*. How had I misread her so badly? We'd had hundreds of conversations while working in the mine. Talking about what we wanted to do once our apprenticeship was over, what kinds of planets and moons and stations we would see, what it would be like to jump in an ocean or watch falling snow. What it would be like to go to a fancy party, or a Hub station, or race in the Diomedes 100. What it would be like to have just one day that we planned entirely by ourselves and took no orders. But no, I thought, it had mostly been me talking. Mae had listened, and complimented, and encouraged me. She *had* encouraged me. But it was because she thought I was talking nonsense. She thought I was just being Cassy with the big imagination and the even bigger mouth, who was going to grow up and get real and marry someone from the cohort and be buried on Aavikko, just like her.

Mae was never going to come with me, I realized numbly. She was right, I had been living in a fantasy world.

I *was* a fool.

But I was a fool with a ship, so there was that.

I stood up. It was time to go.

Contrary to Mae's low evaluation of my planning skills, I had put some thought into this scheme. Inventory shifts had been my favorite and I was good at them. I knew my numbers better than most on Aavikko. I could organize. I could figure out budgets. I could stay afloat. I just needed money.

Good thing there was nearly half a ton of kakorine ore in the storage compartment.

And no, I hadn't stolen it. There was a tiny vein near my site, here in the unowned waste of no-man's land. In fact, it was my primary reason for choosing this site to build. The bit of exposed vein on the surface wasn't much in comparison to what the Company was focused on underground, and 1,000 pounds was nothing compared to what the miners pulled out of the mine every day despite how long it had taken me to gather, but would be enough to keep a small ship both fueled and in funds. And the further we got from Aavikko the more the ore would fetch on the market, which was fine by me.

I had planned to attend the graduation ceremony and say goodbye to everyone, or at least Joren and Big Bihn, but that was no longer an option. I didn't know what Mae was doing right now, but I could see her staging an intervention for my own good. Mae could be unreasonable when it came to rules. Would she rat me out? I had never considered that possibility. But I hadn't expected her to be mad at me. I hadn't expected her to be...offended. If the Company took my ship, I couldn't stop them. There were no other authorities to appeal to. And without *Erebus* the choices for my future were the mine, the raiders, or the slavers.

I would have to be okay with skipping graduation.

The real shame is that I wouldn't be able to shower before I left.

I definitely didn't have enough water on board to waste on bathing, even with the reclamation system working, which it wasn't. I had squirreled away all the water I could, one water skin at a time, until there was enough in the tank to keep two people alive for three weeks. That meant that six weeks was now my deadline for finding a way station, literally.

If this thing could get off the ground in the first place.

"Here goes nothing," I muttered, fastening my harness. I had expected to be nervous, but not like this. I was shaking.

I unhooked my harness, jumped down to the first floor, ran outside, and threw up what little there was in my stomach.

Captain Cassy, daring adventurer.

Wiping my mouth, I climbed back in, did a final system check, and refastened my harness. I could do this. It was like driving the mining drill, but vertical and headed straight into the vacuum of space, right? Yikes. I needed to stop thinking and start doing. I flipped the switch on my armrest and the viewscreen blinked on. All systems were green. I entered a short sequence on the keyboard, took hold of the joystick, and pulled...

There was a heart stopping second of silence.

The engines erupted.

Erebus shook and squealed.

We took-off.

WE TOOK OFF!

The desert rose gently below me, the curve of the planet now clear in the distance. I should have rotated the ship before liftoff, I realized too late, as the individual rock formations melted away into a red sea of sand. I couldn't see Res4.

And then the ship was shaking so hard I thought it would break apart. The atmosphere burned outside as we fought our way through, my teeth rattling loudly in my head. Then, with a jerk that knocked the remaining air from my lungs, we burst into the expanse of open space.

I gasped, coughing, heart pounding in my throat.

Everything was blurry. I rubbed my eyes.

The galaxy spread out before me, a dark, endless tapestry, pinpricks of light glowing in all directions.

And above everything, the giant, swirling purple mass of the Proteus Nebula.

Hands on the joystick, I slowly turned the ship around.

Aavikko was a perfect red sphere. The small rings of white ice around the poles and the wispy ribbons of clouds made it look like a glass marble on a dark floor. I had hoped to see Res4, but there was nothing to see in the flat rusty desert.

In the northern hemisphere, a city was just noticeable from space. That must be Res1. Everyone talked about Res1 like it was enormous, and there it was.

My entire world. I could cover it with my palm.

My plan had worked.

Erebus could fly.

I was free.

Take that, Aavikko!

The artificial gravity had done its job, activating as we broke through the atmosphere. I unhooked my seat restraints and stretched.

It already felt like days since my altercation with Mae, a whole other life, not this same morning.

My stomach growled.

I had about a month's worth of protein bars stored away, received as compensation for extra shifts in the mine. The protein bars were stretching the definition of food, but I wasn't about to starve. I could go down to half rations if things got tight. The limited water supply was a much bigger problem.

I needed to get out of the system. The problem was, I didn't know which direction to go. I didn't even have a map. The Company didn't like those getting around. I knew Aavikko was in the Sector 3 Outskirts, or the 3Out, as we called it, but that was about it. My plan was to follow the nearest short range trading vessel until we reached a stop, then trade for food, water, and a hook-up to the veb. Once I was on the veb I could research anything, even star charts and trading routes, at least that's what the travelers said. But looking outside now, the only other ships I could see in orbit were long range vessels, which were possibly headed into deep space, and raider ships, which were generally bad news. Not that I was much of a target.

I blinked and squinted at the viewscreen. Speaking of raider ships, was that big silver one getting closer?

As if in slow motion, a white blot of light erupted from the bulbous ship. It crawled towards me, picking up speed as it approached until it was just a blinding streak. In my shock, I didn't even get my hands on the joystick before the bolt rushed past, missing the *Erebus* by millimeters. I thought I felt it graze us.

The cockpit speaker burst to life.

"THIS IS THE WARSHIP CLOTILDA. SURRENDER TO THE MIGHT OF THE CALABIAN RAIDERS. WE WILL ISSUE NO FURTHER WARNINGS. PREPARE—"

I hit the kill switch. Uh oh.

Another bolt of light erupted from the ship. This time I was ready, swerving the *Erebus* hard to the left. The bolt still passed far too close.

"Now what?" I cried.

"Do you require navigational guidance?" asked a metallic male voice from the speaker above me.

I jumped. "Hello? Who's that?"

"I am your pilot interface entity. Do you require navigational guidance?"

"Yes!" I yelled. "Get me out of here!"

There was a brief moment of silence as another beam of light crept out of the *Clotilda,* and then I was slammed against my seat as the ship sprang to life, nimbly dodging the bolt. The enormous vessel was a split-second blur on my right as the stars melted around me, a forceful wave tearing at my body.

I was flung from the chair and hurled face first into darkness.

I woke slowly, the feeling of cold metal grating under my cheek sending confused messages to my groggy brain. I opened one eye and found myself staring at a tumble of wires. I was under the captain's chair. The captain's chair...

I was in the *Erebus*. In space. Alive.

"Oh my god!" I sat up, hitting my head on the chair and falling back to the floor with a thud. "Ooooohhh my face! What happened?"

"I interpreted your command as a jump request. Was that an acceptable interpretation of your intent?"

I rubbed my face. My hand came away bloody. Everything hurt. On top of that, my mind was reeling over the fact I had somehow missed this *huge* modification to the XKPR-9 engine. "Yes, thank you." I blew a clot of blood out of my nose, wincing as it splattered across the floor, "I didn't know the engine had a jump drive."

"The engine has significant unadvertised upgrades."

"Like you?" I asked, still piecing together what happened. "What did you call yourself again?"

"I am a pilot interface entity."

"Are you...an artificial intelligence?"

"Yes."

"This is incredible," I said in amazement, shaking my head then immediately regretting it as my eyes swam with stars. I had never met an AI before. "What should I call you?" I croaked.

There was a long pause. *"I have no designation other than Pilot Interface Entity,"* it said eventually, sounding slightly confused.

"That's not going to work," I said, rubbing my face aggressively as I tried to get my vision to clear. "Pilot Interface Entity... Hey! That shortens to P.I.E. Like pie, you know? I'll call you Pie."

There was another moment of silence, then the metallic voice replied slowly, *"My full official designation is Pilot Interface Entity, Prototype Theta, 903BX4—"*

"We don't need to be official," I interrupted, dragging myself onto all fours, then giving a weak laugh. "This isn't really an official operation, if you haven't noticed."

The metallic voice said dryly, *"If official designations are meaningless on this vessel, then I will refer to you as Burrito."*

I blinked in surprise, pausing my crawl across the floor. "Excuse me?"

"Yes, Burrito?"

"Is this for real?" I muttered. "Why are you calling me that?"

*"It makes as much sense as calling **me** Pie."*

My head was hurting too much for this. "Okay, fine. Let's try this again. If I call you...umm...Pilot, will you call me Captain?"

"Yes, Captain."

I gave my face another rub and began the slow and painful process of getting to my feet. "Thank you, Pilot. Now where are we?"

"Hub Chiba," the metallic voice responded promptly. *"The largest space station within the range of a single jump. We need to refuel. The jump depleted all the kakorine loaded into the engine. We are running on fumes."*

"Hub Chiba? Perfect! We need suppli—" I broke off as my eyes focused on the view screen. Where moments before Aavikko sat round and red in the sky, there now hung an enormous, egg-shaped, blue and white space station. I gasped.

Outside zipped ships of every description. Traders, large, small, and every size in between, zoomed on a hundred different tasks, docking at one port then another. Yachts, luxury cruisers, GSTs, and Sector 2 military ships were dotted around, as were security vessels that were painted the same blue and white as the station. I pulled myself into the captain's chair, eyes wide.

"Pilot, look!" Cruising by was an electric yellow, one-man racing ship, with the number 64 painted on the side in black letters that glittered under the lights of the station. "It's one of the Diomedes 100! Wait...is that...?"

"The Tachi-Machi," replied Pilot. *"Finisher 64 in the 2472 race, captained by Zipper Fanshee."*

My jaw dropped. "No way."

Zipper Fanshee was a local celebrity. We didn't watch much live broadcasting on Aavikko, but during the race, the holoscreen in the mess hall was tuned in 25/7, commercials included. Most of the ad time was taken by high budget spots out of Sectors 1 and 2, but a certain amount of time was set aside for local Sector 3 commercials. And as one of the few real celebrities from Sector 3, Zipper happily endorsed products ranging from engine greaser to instant bread to skin cream. He must be here preparing for the next race. It was only a couple weeks away, and Hub Chiba hosted sign-ups. That was really the only thing I knew about the station.

My attention was distracted by a cluster of ships appearing from a jump. They looked like battle cruisers, but I didn't see any mercenary, slaver, or raider branding on the hulls.

"Pilot, are there any raider ships around here?"

"Negative. Hub Chiba does not give clearance to disruptive elements."

Excellent. No more surprise attacks. "Request to dock," I ordered excitedly. "I want to look around."

There was a pause, then a speaker crackled to life and a woman's voice spoke in the bright tones of a service worker.

"Welcome to Hub Chiba, the shining star of the Cymbeline Region. How may I help you?"

"Hello," I said, trying to pitch my voice low and calm, an experienced captain on a routine mission. "I would like to...dock...please."

"Hub Chiba has 14 terminals, all suited to different needs. Which terminal do you desire?"

"Umm...I'm looking to trade and do some shopping?" I volunteered.

"Worker grade or luxury grade?" asked the pleasant voice.

I thought for a second. "Both?"

"Do you require overnight accommodation?"

"Um, no, probably not. I can sleep on my ship."

"Terminal 10 is our multi-audience retail and entertainment level, and should suit your needs. If you desire to re-dock at another terminal, simply reconnect and I will assist you. Additionally, from inside the station, you will have free movement between terminals via our pneumatic tube system. Please enjoy your stay at Hub Chiba!"

The speaker crackled out. Pilot must have received docking instructions, because the *Erebus* started moving towards the smaller end of the station. As we slowly made our way between vessels, I stared out the view screen, still not quite believing what was happening.

I was docking at a space station.

"This is the best moment of my life," I said, reverently.

"*Acknowledged*," said Pilot.

We flew towards the station, which must be nearly as large as Aavikko, until I was nervous about a collision. Then a panel blinked out of existence, revealing a greenish forcefield. I had seen small forcefields used in the mine, but I had never seen one on this scale. *Erebus* passed through the barrier and I felt a hum slide disconcertingly through my body. We entered a shuttle bay containing a dozen or so other personal transports and settled somewhat awkwardly on the grated metal floor. The force field blinked solid.

I was out of the ship in seconds, pausing only to shove as much ore into my bag as I could comfortably carry.

I was stopped at the entrance of the bay by an automated attendant that gave me a list of station rules, informed me that if I failed to pay the 5 buk a day docking fee my ship would be impounded, and gave me a chip that would let me back into the bay. *"Do not lose your chip,"* the machine intoned seriously. *"It is your key to docking bay 10-23. Enjoy your stay on Hub Chiba."*

The door to the station slid open.

I blinked.

There was a riot of color. Glowing. Sparking. Flashing. Exploding. Neon signs flashed from all sides. Dumplings! yelled a sign in bright red. Pastry! screamed a sign in pink. A mass of yellow noodles was being eaten by an animated blue animal who lifted a grinning face to declare YUM in orange capitals. There were also people, hundreds of them, bustling around, eating, shouting, haggling. They were as bright as the signs. A woman floated by in a cascade of blue silk, head shaved, eyes lined in heavy gold. Behind her was a couple wearing matching pink kimonos, sharing a cone of glittering candy and laughing as they passed.

And then the smells hit. Salty, sweet, spicy, hot...could you smell hot? The mess hall never smelled like this. My stomach lurched with hunger.

I stepped into the corridor and was immediately swept into the crowd. A chattering group of what appeared to be 'business people' in white suits appeared from nowhere, pushing me down the hallway, past the stalls of drool-inducing food, around a turn, then deposited me as quickly as they had swept me up.

I blinked again.

I was in a room larger than any I had ever seen. Above me crossed dozens of walkways and large tubes, through which I could see the shadows of people being transported. This was the lowest level and the most crowded, with what must be a thousand people milling about, chatting, eating, pushing, arguing, and laughing, dressed in every color imaginable. There were more people than I had seen in my life. There were more people than the entire population of Res4. A man walked by with blue skin. I stared. Then I noticed a large flashing billboard: *"Past pink? Bored of brown? Try SkinYou, and the rainbow is yours!"*

Fascinated, I walked towards the billboard, but halfway there I was distracted by a shop. In the window was a single leather purse, no larger than my hand. Intrigued, I bent down to read the sign.

"100% authentic human skin purse. Source: Koko Shanel (cert. cloned)."

That was human skin?

I straightened, grimacing.

"You like Koko?" A voice behind me said, causing me to jump and turn around. A man in a well-fitting suit and a poorly fitting face offered me a smile. He gestured at the purse.

"Um, no, I'm just browsing. Excuse me," I said, moving quickly back into the crowd.

"BEEEEEEP!!!!!" I jumped, narrowly avoiding a collision. A gorilla in a red jacket zoomed by on an electric scooter, grunting and weaving through the crowd. They took a moment to turn and shake a gloved fist in my direction before disappearing into the sea of people.

Feeling overwhelmed, I moved back into the crush, letting the tides pull me towards another atrium. This space was similar to the first, but dominated by an enormous banner reading, *"The Diomedes 100 — Become A Champion!"* Below, a slightly smaller font read, *"Sign-Up are NOW OPEN until the start of the race. Good luck to our future 100!"*

I stopped and stared at the sign, transfixed.

This was where the best pilots in the galaxy registered for the Diomedes 100. And I was here too.

Pinch me.

The realization of where I was, what I had just done, washed over me. My vision was suddenly blurry.

I had done it.

I had a new life.

Taking a deep breath, I steadied myself. Things weren't going to be easy; I knew that. But despite being a stranger here, I knew the important things. For one, I knew the language. Some places in Sector 1 and even Sector 2 used regional languages, but everyone in Sector 3 spoke Comglish. Another positive was that all of Sector 3 used buks. I wouldn't have to figure out a currency exchange. And lastly, kakorine was popular and the only fuel source used in jump drives, so my inventory should be easy to shift. There was a lot in my favor. I could do this.

I must have been buffed into a side passage while thinking, because suddenly I was in a less crowded area next to a large sign that read TRASH. There were chutes in the walls for waste removal but also enormous bins for larger items. I walked over, curious to what scrap looked like on a space station. Standing next to the bins were two men and a woman, notably dirtier and shabbier than the other people I'd seen on Hub Chiba. The men were skinny but the woman was fat. There wasn't enough food on Aavikko for anyone but the management to get fat, but even they didn't get *this* fat. If not for the rest of her appearance I would have assumed she was extremely wealthy. The trio waved at me. Confused, I waved back and cautiously moved closer.

"Hi," I said.

"Hi," replied one of the men. He had the same accent as the travelers from the Imago cluster. "Haven't seen you before. Which terminal are you from?"

I shook my head. "I just got here. I'm from Aavikko."

The men looked confused, but the woman looked at me with interest, sniffing the air in my direction. "The mining planet?" Then she laughed, her face dissolving into cheerful wrinkles. "Boys, she's not homeless. She's a sand-eater. That's planet dirt."

"Shit, I thought you were a station rat," said the first guy, looking me up and down. "But you're right, that's planet dirt. What on Chiba are you doing here?"

I gave them my biggest smile. Time to get to work. "I'm looking to sell some unrefined kakorine ore — great quality, low prices. You know anyone who would be interested?"

The group exchanged looks. This is not what they had been expecting.

"I'll give you 10%."

This got their attention. The first man looked at me appraisingly, "How much have you got?"

"Enough for a couple small trades, nothing fancy," I replied casually. "Are you interested? Just introduce me to some buyers."

"Unrefined kakorine?" He looked pensive. "Yeah, I know some shops that run on that. But if you want my connections, you'll have to give me 50%."

"It was nice talking to you," I said and turned to walk away. This was just like negotiating on Aavikko. I had only taken a couple steps when I heard him call out to me.

"Wait!"

I turned around.

He was grinning. "40%," he said.

I walked back towards the group. "15."

"30."

"20."

"25," he said and raised an eyebrow.

I stuck out my fist. "25."

We pounded fists.

"Okay," said the man. "I'll show you around. My name is Rhodri, by the way. And this is Buzz and Roxie."

"I'm Cassy," I said.

Rhodri led me out of the trash area and down a smaller hallway full of junk shops. We ducked into a store that seemed to specialize in used power converters and glowing buttons of dancing cats.

The man behind the counter was busy with a half-woman. I blinked and looked again. Floating in front of me was a woman with no legs, resting on a hovering platform about three feet off the floor. As the man behind the counter gestured to something on the wall behind him, the floating woman gracefully moved a few inches to the left to get a better view.

When people lost their legs on Res4 they usually died. If not, they were propped up in a chair and given monitor duty.

I realized I was staring and quickly moved my eyes to the merchandise. It was mostly the kind of cheap trinkets that were often off-loaded on Res4. I saw some blue hair ribbons I had given to Mae for her last birthday.

"Hey Balmeet!" called Rhodri to a small man behind the counter, causing me to jump. The floating woman had silently left the store. "You still running that old kakorine generator?"

Balmeet nodded.

"How much are they ripping you off for ore?"

Balmeet shrugged. "There's no rip off. Just 50 buks a pound."

I felt my eyes go wide and quickly put back on my sales face. On Res4 the Company sold direct unrefined ore for 20 buks a pound, and they sometimes took 15. We must have jumped further than I thought for prices to be this high.

I had to take a closer look at that engine.

"Well, it's your lucky day!" Rhodri was saying. "This is my friend Cassy, and she's got insider connections."

"Pleased to meet you, Balmeet," I said with a smile. "What would you say to 5 pounds of kakorine at 45 buks a pound?"

Balmeet considered me for a moment, eyes skeptical, then shrugged again. "45 buks? Sounds low quality."

I dug in my bag and pulled out a small piece, tossing it to him. He caught it and held it up to the light, pulled a face, then nodded. "Okay. I will give you 200 buks for 5 pounds."

"215," I said, and stuck out my fist. He thought for a moment, looked at Rhodri, shrugged a final time, and pounded.

I had just made my first off-world deal.

Exiting the shop and feeling generous, I handed 60 buks to Rhodri. "You have any more friends?"

He grinned at the money. "You bet!"

Thirty minutes and four stalls later I had unloaded the last of my ore and had nearly 1,000 buks in my pocket. It was more money than I had seen in my entire life.

"Don't flash your buks around, kid," Rhodri said, giving me a nudge. "Put them away. And you should probably be a little less trusting in the future. This station is pretty safe but there are still people that will knife you for a buk."

I gave him a sidewise glance. "You gonna rob me?"

He laughed. "No way. I'm a pacifist. Anyway, if I wanted you dead it would have happened already."

"That's comforting."

"You hungry?"

"Yeah!"

As we walked back to the restaurant district, I asked curiously, "Are you guys...homeless? You, Buzz, and Roxie, I mean. I would have thought everyone on Chiba would have somewhere to sleep. I mean, this place is really nice."

Rhodri laughed, "Nah, I'm not homeless. Well," he scratched his head, "I guess that depends on what you mean. I don't have a *permanent* residence, that's true. I used to, but it just seemed like a hassle and waste of money. I'm a porter on the monthly transport to the Imago cluster, so I'm only here one week a month anyway. It's safe enough on this level of the station, especially if you have a few people to hang with. I have a locker for my things and a good bedroll, so I'm happy. I would rather save my money for when I can't make it anymore."

"What about Roxie?" I asked.

"I wouldn't call her homeless. She has kids on the station she could stay with if she wanted to. I think she technically owns her daughter's place on level 2, but the place is full of babies and she can't stand babies. There's another daughter on level 8 with an insufferable husband, so she won't stay there, and another son on level 14 with a husband she adores, and she wants to keep it that way so she won't stay with them either. But no, I wouldn't call her proper homeless. She's just doing things differently these days."

"What about Buzz?"

"Oh, Buzz is a station rat. Nice guy though."

We bought four bowls of spicy noodles and brought them back to the trash area to eat with the others. The four of us circled up behind the largest bin, sat down on broken crates, and dug into the rich steaming broth. I couldn't remember anything ever tasting so good.

I let myself relax against the smooth wall of the bin, satiated and happy. Everything was going smoothly.

Famous last words.

Chapter 5
The Nibiru Club

Six hours later I walked through the red crystal door of the Nibiru Club, the hottest club on Hub Chiba, my hair clean and shining, my skin glowing like polished bronze under my filmy white dress.

Trying not to feel like an imposter, I scanned the room for the bar.

The rest of the day had been a whirlwind. After lunch, my new friends wanted to nap but I was buzzing with excitement. Saying I would see them later, I headed out to do some shopping.

My first stop was new clothes, and not just for vanity. It was pretty clear I looked worse than a vagrant by Chiba standards, and that was a problem if I wanted to be taken seriously as a trader. I ducked into a hardware store and bought a small backpack to replace my canvas sack, sturdy hemp boots, and three new jumpsuits in blue, red, and green. This amused me. On Res4, jumpsuit color indicated position and rank. I was now a full member of the Company and a foreman in both power generation and waste disposal. Congratulations, me.

Next, I set off to find a bath. There were signs for two buk showers, which seemed like a good option until I passed the first spa. The deal on the window read: *SPECIAL! Shower ☼ tub soak ☼ body scrub ☼ hair wash, cut, and blow-dry ☼ PLUS manicure and pedicure! 15 buks today only!*

I didn't know what some of those words meant, but it seemed like an impressive list. Looking at my reflection in the spa's window, covered in sand and dirt, streaked with tear stains, and with a smear of blood running from my nose to my ear, I decided to do myself, and everyone else, a favor.

Pushing through the heavy wooden doors, I was immediately whisked away by a pair of loincloth-wearing attendants with glittering gold skin. They held me at an arm's length and ordered me to strip, then carried away my clothes with noses pinched.

"Will I get those back?" I asked after them.

"No," they replied in unison, sounding horrified.

The shower and soak that followed were like a dream. The idea of sitting in clean water just because it felt good was madness. Beautiful, wonderful, madness. *Sitting* in clean water? With your butt? Incredible. The haircut, manicure, and pedicure weren't nearly as pleasant, with the attendants rolling their eyes at my scalp and the dirt under my nails, but I couldn't criticize the results. After changing into my new green jumpsuit, I was confident I would no longer be confused with a "station rat."

My next stop was a normal clothing store. I was mostly curious about what people wore around here, where clothes weren't assigned. I wandered through the racks, brushing my hands across the soft clothing. Floating, draping fabrics seemed to be popular. I looked down at my stiff jumpsuit. Maybe I should buy something else.

As if reading my mind, a pale saleswoman with heavily lined eyes appeared at my elbow. "Let me guess," she said, putting a long, black-nailed finger to her lips. "First time on the station and you need something to wear to the Nibiru Club? Am I right?"

I shrugged, "I guess..."

"I knew it!" she clasped her hands, "I have just the dress. As soon as I saw you, I knew it was yours. It's *perfect* for you."

A soft white dress appeared from nowhere and I was pushed into a dressing room. I had to admit, the lady knew her stuff. The dress slid over me like liquid, hitting above my knee and leaving one shoulder exposed. I looked like Queen Kelopatra in the Earth's Avengers holo series, I thought with surprise. I looked pretty good.

The saleswoman stepped back with an admiring nod. "Not many with an athletic build like that around here," she said, poking my arm. "Such muscle definition!"

"Thanks," I said, awkwardly.

She made the sale. I even bought sandals to match.

I headed back to the *Erebus,* stopping briefly along the way to pick up toiletries, clean underwear, and pay the docking fee to the attendant. It only took a minute to hide the bulk of my newly acquired wealth in a storage compartment, shove my docking pass and money into my new backpack, and head back out. I was tired, but my dress deserved to see the Nibiru Club.

And here I was. The first day of the rest of my life. I took a step forward.

SLAM!

I collided with a tall figure. He yelled "oof" and stumbled backwards, holding his chest and wheezing. "Man down!" he gasped theatrically.

"You ran into me!" I yelled back, then blinked in surprise. "Oh!"

The man in front of me was Zipper Fanshee.

He stood there, eyeing me with annoyance, his two-meter frame adorned by a red bandleader's jacket, gold buttons glowing, black pompadour crowning his angular face.

He definitely had a look.

Zipper Fanshee was the only captain from the 3Out, to ever, and I mean *ever*, race in the Diomedes 100. And he placed. He had a number. He was a hero.

And a bit of a heart throb.

I wasn't sure how old he was but he couldn't be that much older than me. It wasn't so long ago he was considered a kid wonder, back when he competed in the lower-stakes feeder races. Now he had a small veb empire with a massive following here on Chiba, according to the trader gossip.

And he was even cuter than I expected. Mae used to say that things were guaranteed to look shinier in the holos than real life, but maybe that wasn't always the case.

"Alright then," he said, straightening his jacket. "I *suppose* we ran into each other."

"That seems fair," I said, smiling. This was surreal.

He smiled back, not his signature toothy grin but a normal, friendly smile. "You're from Aavikko, aren't you? I like your accent. It's nice to hear someone local — this place is getting overrun with people from Sector 2."

"Zipper?" A small group of people had gathered behind him, datapads out for photos and autographs. Several of them were wearing replicas of Zipper's racing goggles, and a toothy girl in front was clutching a pad of paper and a retro ink pen with a topper shaped like Zipper's pompadour.

"I think your fan club found you," I said, fascinated.

He nodded ruefully, then turned to greet his admirers. "Hi, friends!" I heard him say in an overly bright voice.

I continued towards the bar, beaming to myself. First day off planet and I already met a celebrity? Mae would freak. My grin faltered. Why did I keep thinking of her?

A waiter walked by with a tray of promotional drinks, Fin's Gin, infused with silverleaf and the best in Sector 3, according to the label. I grabbed a glass and saddled up to an empty cocktail table. I needed to focus on having a good time. Right.

I took a sip of the gin. It was pretty good. Didn't burn as much as that stuff Tim brewed behind the tavern.

The room was dimly illuminated by a sparkling white vapor that hung in the air in glittering ribbons. Blue lights rimmed the walls, giving the room the impression of being underwater. In the middle of the floor was the bar, a glowing circle full of white suited bartenders skillfully juggling bottles.

On the other side of the bar was the dance floor, blasting ambient, neoclassical house music. It was early, but the floor was already filling with people of all shapes, sizes, and colors. I caught a glimpse of someone covered with tiger stripes.

It should have been enough to fully capture my attention, but instead I found myself going back over the events of the morning. Today had been an extremely lucky day for me, but I shouldn't have needed *that* much luck. Raider ships don't start fights in Aavikko orbit. They just don't. Sure, Aavikko didn't have any planetary defenses, but that's because it didn't need them. Aavikko protected itself. Aavikko was the only stop for cheap kakorine in the whole Cymbeline Region. And it was *very* cheap. I had no idea how cheap until today. I still couldn't believe it was selling for 50 buks a pound as close as Hub Chiba, but then again, I wasn't entirely sure where Chiba was. I needed to get a map.

The point was, everyone knew that direct sales were against the Company's corporate policy. But everyone also knew that Corporate, based in their big shiny tower back on Earth, turned a blind eye to their farthest outpost as long as there wasn't any trouble. It was in the region's best interest to keep Aavikko safe. Safe meant unregulated.

And yet a Calabrian ship risked opening fire on a crappy tin can right above Res4? In order to get one random slave?

I had no idea what to do with that. I should probably order a drink. I looked over at the bar, squinting to read the specials.

A man was sitting at the bar, partially blocking the menu. I stared.

I had never seen white skin like his before. Not like that. I was one of the paler people on Res4, but my skin wasn't really white. It was brownish with freckles that would make me darker than Joren if they ever spread. It was the color of used engine oil.

This man was *white*. Like bleached paper. My mind went to a holo I had seen years ago about vampires. They drank blood but had none of their own. That holo had gotten unexpectedly erotic halfway through and management had shut it off. They didn't like us getting worked up during meals.

The man was watching the crowd with the air of an emperor surveying his subjects. He raised a small glass of an amber liquid to his lips.

Our eyes met.

An almost imperceptible smile flicked across his face, and he held my gaze as he finished his sip. Then he set down his glass and walked over.

"There was still booze in that glass," I said as he approached.

"I'll buy another," he said, coming to a stop. He put his hand on the table. "What are you drinking?"

I didn't know any fancy drinks. "Same as you."

He held up two fingers, his eyes flicking to a nearby waiter. The waiter gave him a nod and hurried off.

"Mal," he said by way of introduction.

"Cassy," I replied.

"So, what are you here to escape?" he asked with an air of practiced boredom as he scanned the room over my left shoulder.

What an odd thing to say. "This is me escaped," I said. "I've never been here before."

He looked back at me, slightly amused. "That explains the enthusiasm. Try not to look too impressed."

I couldn't help but laugh. "So why are *you* here, if it's so unimpressive?"

"I came here to relax," he said. "And get some perspective. I've been wrapped up in my work recently." He tapped his fingers against the table. "I'm on the edge of a major breakthrough."

"What kind?"

He gave me an evaluating look and then shrugged, as if deciding I was harmless. "Have you ever had a dream? Something you wanted so badly you would do anything for it?"

"Sure," I said, honestly.

He raised an eyebrow. "I mean a real dream. Something big. Something that takes imagination and bravery."

"Yes," I repeated.

"No," he said, patiently, "I mean something that puts life in perspective. Something that raises you above the day-to-day nonsense that distracts most people."

"Totally," I said, nodding, "Like I always say, sleep tight and dream big, the rocks might crush you tomorrow!"

There was a moment of silence.

"You're not from around here, are you." It wasn't a question.

"What gave me away?" I grinned. "No, I just got here this morning."

An odd, thoughtful look passed across his pale face, "Your accent — are you from Aavikko?"

I knew I had an accent, but I didn't realize it was *that* strong. "Yeah, Res4."

"I've heard of Res4," he said, slowly, "That's the town with the scrap trade."

"Yup, I had a sideline scraping. Lots of people there do. Well, not Mae, she didn't like it, but..." I trailed off.

He was looking at me as if I had grown another head and sprouted wings. "*You* just arrived from Aavikko? You wouldn't be the new arrival in Bay 10-23, would you?"

It was my turn to be surprised. "Yeah, I guess? How did you know that?"

The waiter came back, deftly depositing two drinks before floating away.

Mal glanced at the departing figure, then paused, his attention arrested by something behind me. "Is that Zipper Fanshee?"

I turned my head, following his gaze to the clump of people near the door, "Yeah, it is. I bumped into him earlier. I think his fan club is based here."

Mal nodded distractedly and handed me one of the glasses, then held up his drink in a toast.

"To achieving goals, one way or another," he said, drinking.

I held the glass up in acknowledgement and took a quick sip, then repeated, "How did you know where I'm docked?"

Mal swirled the amber liquid, "Lucky guess, mostly. There aren't many new arrivals in Terminal 10 on Tuesday mornings. I was walking by the bay when there was an announcement that the forcefield was down for an arrival. I'm docked in Bay 10-24."

"You have a ship?" I asked, immediately interested. "What kind?"

"XTX Falcon, Starslip edition." He raised a self-satisfied eyebrow at me, daring me to be impressed.

I was impressed. "A Falcon Starslip? Like Captain Ace?"

He laughed. "You know your ships. Are you an Ace fangirl? Yes, Captain Ace flew a Starslip, but the CTX model."

"Can I see it?" I blurted out. The booze had hit and I was feeling giddy. The Falcon Starslip was my dream ship. And this was a *better* model? I had to see it.

He was looking at me with satisfaction. "Well, aren't we an eager beaver. If you play your cards right, maybe you can see it later."

I resisted the urge to roll my eyes. "What's her name?"

"*The Dreamer*. What's yours?"

"*Erebus*," I said, taking another sip.

He raised an eyebrow. "Air-bus?"

"No!" I laughed and shook my head. "*Erebus*. It's from a holo. Never mind."

"You know," he said, brushing a stray piece of hair out of my face. "You have very beautiful eyes. I don't think I've ever seen gold irises before."

"Thanks," I said. His hand was cold. I pushed it away as politely as possible.

"So, you just arrived? Is it only you on board?" he asked. "Or do you have a crew hanging about?" He looked around in mock suspicion.

"Nope," I said, "It's just me. I was hoping a friend would come too, but that didn't work out. I do have an AI pilot though."

"Oh yes?" he said casually, leaning even closer. He smelled of liquor and sweet perfume. "AI pilots are pretty rare."

I nodded. "Yup. He's, um, useful." Speaking was getting difficult, but I wasn't worried about it. I wasn't worried about anything. The music pulsed through my body. The lights from the dance floor threw rainbows on the far wall. So shiny...

Mal waved a hand in front of my face. "Hello? Are you feeling okay?"

I nodded slowly, eyes still glued on the colorful lights. "Yeah I'm goooooooood." The end of the word turned into a giggle, which was very funny. I laughed at it, which was even funnier. How wonderful everything was! I wanted to dance.

"Dance!" I said, happily.

I was on the floor. I wasn't sure how I got there. Was I dancing? No, this was still the bar. There was gum stuck to the bottom of the table. My legs were in front of me. I could see them but they weren't working. "Move!" I tried to say, but my mouth wasn't working either.

Hands were helping me up. Mal put my arms through the straps of my backpack. "Cassy?" He said from a long way off. "Cassy, I think the whiskey hit you a little hard."

"Humm?" I replied, swinging my head around. My neck felt weird. Was it still my neck? Neck was a weird word. The lights from the dance floor were blinding. I tried to look away but the lights were in my eyes. I rubbed at them.

Mal was still talking, "...this waitress — excuse me, miss? — will take you to the hotel, okay?"

"Hotel?" I repeated in confusion. "No, my...my ship."

My knees stopped working. The barstool caught me. Good barstool.

A member of the waitstaff was standing next to me, a hand under my elbow. "Miss, we're going to have to cut you off. I'll escort you to our club hotel. Malaki has kindly paid for your room tonight. Please come with me."

Malaki?

Mal's pale eyes watched me go. My eyes watched him back, blinking slowly, recording images without comprehension.

We were walking through a doorway. Down a tunnel. A wormhole. The part of my brain still functioning let go.

I was laying down, lights dimming around me. In the fading glow I saw curved walls closing in. I reached out to touch them but the lights were only echoes, and I was in darkness.

And then there was nothing.

Trapped.

Cave in.

Panic rose in my throat. I fought down the wave of nausea and forced myself to breathe.

The rocks were soft under my fingers. I dug in, bracing myself for pain.

The rocks were *very* soft.

Rocks weren't typically soft, were they?

I opened my eyes.

I was staring at a smooth white ceiling about two feet above my face.

This wasn't a cave in.

I blinked again, shaking my head, forcing the world into focus.

There were lights around the edge of the ceiling. They were slowly getting brighter.

Crackle. A spit of static announced that a speaker was activating, then a pleasant female voice spoke soothingly. *"Okite kudasai. It is time for check-out. Please proceed to the front door in an orderly fashion. Thank you for staying at Hotel Kizetsu. We hope to see you again soon."*

I was in a capsule hotel. This was a bed.

Just as I was starting to relax, the wall to my right whooshed open, revealing a hallway full of similarly opening doors.

A split second later, the bed tipped violently sidewise, tossing me into an undignified heap on the floor, my backpack narrowly missing my head.

Around me, the corridor was flooded with people rolling gracefully out of identical bunks, rubbing bleary faces and yawning.

I struggled to my feet, grabbing my bag. Fighting through a vale of dizziness and confusion, I allowed myself to be swept towards the exit, joining the mass shuffling of zombie-like former partygoers. This was apparently normal. No one was giving me a second glance. I just needed to get back to my ship.

The streets were mostly empty, with a trickle of people opening caffeine cafes and running deliveries. It appeared that the station followed a day/night schedule, despite being outside any solar systems, and I guessed it was very early morning. I definitely needed more sleep. It was with great relief that I saw the sign for Bay 10-23.

I reached into my backpack for the key.

It was missing.

Oh no.

I searched again, then dumped the contents of my bag onto the floor.

It was gone.

A sudden wave of nausea passed over me and I had to sit down and take deep breaths to keep from vomiting. Two drinks and this was my hangover? How? And where was my key?

"Long night?" came a voice to my right.

An older woman was walking towards me with an overnight bag slung over her shoulders. She gave me a smile, her face turning into cheerful wrinkles.

"Yeah..." I said, awkwardly sweeping my things back into my bag. "And I managed to lock myself out."

The woman tutted as she swiped her own key. "You have to be careful, my dear. There won't always be someone to let you back in." She gave me a wink as the door slid open.

"Really? Oh, thank you!" I struggled to my feet.

She laughed. "You're lucky I saw you leave yesterday. Don't lose your key again, okay?"

I sincerely promised to be more careful and hurried to *Erebus*, cheeks burning with embarrassment.

Erebus was waiting for me, quiet and familiar.

I breathed a sigh of relief as the door slid shut behind me, the ship's cool interior enveloping my clammy skin. But the feeling of nausea I had woken up with was still twisting in my stomach.

"I need some air," I said to myself. "Let's go for a drive."

I manually refueled the engine with kakorine, crawled into the cockpit, buckled myself into the pilot's seat, and flipped the switches in the pre-flight sequence. Having an AI was cool, but I wanted to fly myself.

"Hey Chiba?" I said over the comm. "I'm going out for a bit. I'm paid up for the night and I'll be back soon."

There was a fractional pause before a bright voice responded, *"Good morning! Your space will be held for 6 hours. Thank you for choosing Hub Chiba!"*

I switched off the comm and put my hands on the controls.

Almost immediately I felt the artificial gravity turn off beneath the ship, the physical connection to the station broken. Activating thrusters, I moved carefully towards the holographic wall that separated the bay from open space.

It wasn't exactly graceful, but I managed to get *Erebus* out without crashing into anything. Only a few dozen small transports were zipping around outside, mostly GSTs like me. It seemed the majority of the station was still asleep.

I pointed the ship towards nothingness and leaned back in my chair, my sore back cracking into place. I hadn't slept very well, but I could afford to catch a quick nap now. After all, I was my own boss.

I curled my feet onto the chair and drifted away.

There was a *clunk.*

I scrunch up my face. That was probably normal.

Clunk clunk

I opened my eyes. No, not normal. "Pilot?"

CLUNCK!

Uh oh.

The acrid smell of burning reached me as the cockpit filled with smoke.

Smoke?!

"Pilot?" I said urgently, waving a hand at the cloudy air and starting to cough. "Pilot! What is going on?"

The back of the ship exploded.

The force of the explosion knocked me forward against my restraints, my head whipping forward painfully. Through the viewscreen I could see pieces of ship flying off, spinning away from us. My ship was disintegrating.

The opening between the cockpit and the rest of the ship hissed shut, sealing me off as the ship shook violently. The emergency protocol had been activated, turning the cockpit into an escape pod.

The cockpit was shaking too.

It wasn't going to hold.

I felt rather than heard a leak spring behind me. A seam had broken.

"Pilot?" I wheezed, the smoke clawing at my throat, choking me. "Please answer!"

This seemed like a good time to panic.

"Hello there, Erebus," said a deep voice through the speaker. *"Do you need a lift?"*

I looked out the window and froze. No way.

Outside was the familiar hull I knew from countless hours of holos. Blue plating gleamed in the light of the station; orange racing stripes blazed like lightning bolts down the enormous rounded sides.

It was Captain Ace.

Captain Ace was rescuing me.

There was an explosion behind me and the cockpit completely disconnected from the body of the ship.

"Come in, Erebus," the masculine voice said with more urgency. The large vessel moved closer.

Was I dreaming? What kind of hangover was this? I shook my head. The smoke filling the cockpit had turned a slimy black.

"Hello?" I croaked.

"There you are!" said the voice. *"Would you like some help?*

"Yes!" I coughed. "Please!"

My eyes were burning. I tried fanning the smoke away from my face, dimly making out the large ship moving closer. There was no more air. I closed my eyes and started to gag.

I couldn't breathe.

There was a scraping noise, then a 'pop'. I felt a *whoosh* of air as the smoke was sucked from the cockpit, and another *whoosh* as fresh, cool air flooded in. I gasped, clean air rushing into my burning lungs. Hands were grabbing me, pulling me from the wreckage, placing me on a cold smooth floor.

It took a moment for my eyes to adjust to the lights. I pushed myself to my feet, wheezing.

There was a man in front of me.

Captain Ace?

I blinked hard and tried again.

Mal was looking down at me with vague amusement.

"You?" I asked, confused.

"Hello Cassy," said Mal. He was elegantly dressed in a tailored white nehru button down and navy slacks, as cool as when I meet him at the bar. "It looks like you've had a bit of an accident."

"Umm...yeah," I said, looking around. Behind me was the wreck of my ship, in pieces on the floor. My eyes filled with hot tears, burning from the smoke. I swallowed sour bile as my stomach twisted. My ship…

Mal looked at me sympathetically. "Come with me — I'll take you to a guest room to clean up. This must be a shock."

I nodded, but my attention was diverted by the dozen or so other people in the room. They were gathering up the pieces of my ship. Smaller pieces were going into wheeled bins, while larger pieces were fixed with anti-gravity pads and levitated away.

"They are just moving it to a better place," said Mal, following my gaze.

The better place seemed to be a red, mid-sized racing ship, the only other thing in the cavernous docking bay. I couldn't see it clearly. My eyes were still burning.

"What happened?" I tried to say, but the attempt just triggered another choking fit.

"Maybe you shouldn't talk right now," Mal said, soothingly.

I nodded, coughing.

Hand on my shoulder, he steered me out of the shuttlebay and into a long, gleaming corridor. It looked just like the Captain Ace holos. Any other time I would be excited, but right now I was still trying to get the smoke out of my face. He led me down the hall, then down another identical hall, and then another.

"Where are we going?" I finally managed to croak.

"Here," he said, stopping in front of a door and hitting a button. It whooshed open to reveal a bedroom furnished with expensive looking furniture.

"Please, make yourself at home," said Mal, gesturing for me to enter.

I stepped inside. In the center of the room was a huge bed with a fluffy white comforter. It looked very inviting.

"Thanks," I whispered.

"Why don't you clean up and get some rest. There is water in the bathroom," he said, gesturing to a small door in the wall, "and I'll bring some food in a bit. Then we can figure out what to do with you, okay? That was a very close call."

"Yeah," I said, starting to catch my breath. My head was still spinning. "It was. Thanks again. I...I don't know what I would have done if you hadn't been there."

Mal gave me a small smile, then turned and left the room. The door slid shut behind him.

I was alone.

As soon as he was gone, I flopped onto the bed, the tears I had been holding back flowing freely.

Couldn't anything go right? I pulled the comforter over my head, burrowing into the bed. The mattress was incredibly soft. If I laid there any longer I would probably cry myself to sleep.

I shouldn't do that.

Despite my exhaustion, I forced myself to my feet. I could rest after I figured out what happened. *Erebus* would tell me. The damage had looked pretty bad when I saw it in the bay, but Mal had at least collected the pieces for me. Maybe this was fixable. I had to stay positive and focused. I hadn't spent all those years building a ship to give up now.

I walked over to the door, expecting it to automatically open in front of me. It didn't. I reached out and hit the panel next to the door. Still nothing.

"Hey ship?" I said. "Please open my door?"

Silence.

"Door open!" I commanded.

Nothing.

"OPEN NOW!" I shouted.

The door was locked.

Uh oh.

Trapped again.

I started pacing, blood rushing to my head.

Why was the door locked?

There could be good reasons, I told myself. Tons of reasons. Reasons like...

Uhhh...

My heart was pounding in my ears.

Why was the door locked?

Where did my shuttlebay key go?

Why did *Erebus* fall apart?

I stopped pacing. This was wrong.

I had to get away. Now.

My survival instincts were screaming.

What would Captain Ace do?

I took a deep breath. That wasn't such a bad question. What *would* Captain Ace do? Not have a panic attack, that's for sure. Ace wouldn't be phased about a locked door, especially on a Falcon. He knew how to sneak around the entire *Kitty Leroy* without being caught.

When pirates took over in the season two finale he crawled through the ventilation ducts to escape, coming back with a full crew of his own to retake the ship in the season three premiere. It was very exciting, but that couldn't actually work, right?

Out of curiosity, I pulled the dresser away from the wall.

Behind it was a small metal grate.

No way.

NO WAY.

I grabbed my hairpin, dropped to my knees, and went to work on the screws. It took a few minutes, but I got all four screws out and pulled the grate to the floor.

Behind it was a long, dark passage, just wide enough for my shoulders. There was no way that a big guy like Captain Ace could fit.

But I could.

I stared at the hole.

There was still a chance that I was freaking out over nothing and everything was fine.

Except nothing was fine. *Erebus* was gone and I *knew* it wasn't because I'd messed up. She would have fallen apart during the jump. There was no way a ship that could make a jump would fall apart while peacefully floating around doing literally nothing. It didn't make sense.

And Mal had been right there to swoop me up. What a coincidence.

Mae sometimes accused me of being paranoid. But I was reasonably sure this wasn't paranoia.

I hadn't left Aavikko to get locked in some dude's guest room.

I dropped to my hands and knees and entered the crawl space.

The long passage was dimly illuminated by grates in the wall, offering slitted views into other cabins. The first several grates opened into similar bedrooms, empty, but clearly occupied by the permanent crew. Posters hung on walls and clothes were tossed across unmade beds. Normal stuff. After a few similar rooms I started feeling silly. Maybe I could make it back to my room before Mal returned. This would be embarrassing to explain.

Just then I reached a T and paused, listening. A babble of voices was coming from the left-hand passage. Deciding to push on, I headed towards the sound until I reached another grate, then stopped and peered through.

I was looking into the mess hall. There were a few rows of tables and the back wall was lined with appliances and food storage cabinets. About a dozen people were milling about and chatting.

"...here now, in the guest room," a hulking man with a heavily scarred face was saying angrily. "How many girls are we going to pick up? This is not part of the plan!"

One of his companions opened his mouth to speak, but broke off as the door to the mess hall opened. Malaki walked in.

The staff scrambled to sit down as he took his place at the front of the room.

"Listen up," he said. "We are one big step closer to our goal."

There was a round of scattered applause. Malaki held up a hand and the room fell silent.

"We'll have plenty of time to celebrate after we win." He turned to look at the man with the scarred face. "Kven, what's the status of the AI?"

"It's been installed on the racer," he responded gruffly. "The engineers said it was easy, despite the hack job getting it out. And the rest of the girl's wreck is in the racer's storage hold."

Pilot? Were they talking about Pilot?

"Good," said Mal. "Is the racer ready to go?"

Kven nodded, "She's fueled and stocked."

Malaki looked pleased. "Excellent. At last, things are coming together. And the slingshot?"

A man with long pale hair and dark glasses shook his head. "Still doing final testing. But it will be ready by the race, my guarantee."

"Boss?" said Kven. "The crew has been wondering, now that we have the AI, are we getting paid?"

"You will be paid *after* the race, as promised," Mal said.

"Yeah, but boss," Kven continued, "we still haven't gotten that bonus we were supposed to get after the tech came through in the first place."

Mal's pale eyes narrowed. "You know the reason for that. This isn't the time to argue, Kven. We are days away from all that money and more. Understand?" His tone brooked no argument. "Any more questions?"

The crew exchanged looks. The money question was clearly the one they had been most interested in. After a pause, a fat man raised his hand cautiously, "What's the plan for the new girl?"

Malaki shrugged. "She is a complication, but hopefully a minor one. She believes her ship fell apart on its own, which is hardly a stretch. It looked like it was assembled from a trash heap."

The crew sniggered. I clenched my jaw. My ship *had* been assembled from a trash heap.

"She shouldn't cause you any problems," Malaki was saying. "She was eating out of my hand last night, and that was before I saved her life. As far as she's concerned, she owes us. We'll keep her around for now. We can always get rid of her later."

He said that casually, like it was the most natural thing in the world. Get rid of her.

Get rid of *me*.

"It was a stroke of luck, meeting her at the club," he continued. "Retrieving the AI before her ship left Chiba has put us ahead of schedule."

"Boss?" Another member of the crew raised his hand. "Not to question, but why bring her on board at all?"

"'Cause she's fit," interjected the fat man with a grin.

"For a sand-eater!" yelled someone in the back. The crew laughed.

Malaki gave a thin smile and held up a finger for silence. "Her ship fell apart so quickly that Chiba security was already enroute, so she would have been rescued regardless. This way, *they* thanked *us* for helping out. And we were able to claim her wreckage, on the off-chance Tef squirreled away more surprises." He shrugged, as if the difference in plans was negligible. "I'm sure the girl can make herself useful. She'll keep the kid company if nothing else." He glanced at the large clock on the wall. "That's everything. I'm going to stop by engineering, then check on our guest. Enjoy your breakfast. We'll start engine tests at 1300." The rest of the crew immediately hopped up and started passing out plates and utensils with practiced efficiency. Chow time. Business as usual.

From my hiding spot in the crawl space, I crouched in silence. Malaki had tried to kill me. Why? I didn't understand what was going on. But I did know one thing: last night Mal had put something in my drink and taken my shuttlebay key. While I was unconscious in that weird hotel, he had cut Pilot out of my ship.

I had been completely played.

Inside the mess hall, the crew was starting to eat. I had a sliver of time before Malaki checked on me, but I had to move *right now*.

Trusting that the sound of clinking dishes would cover any sounds from the vent, I started crawling again, this time faster. In the Captain Ace holos, the shuttlebay was on the same floor as the mess hall, on the opposite end of the ship from the bunk rooms. And so far, the holos were proving pretty accurate. I crawled for a good couple minutes and was starting to be concerned by the lack of grates when I saw light coming through a vent in the wall. I slid up next to the opening and peered out.

I had found the shuttlebay.

It was empty save for the racer. I studied it for a moment. I didn't recognize the model, suggesting a custom build. She was about ten times the size of *Erebus*, sleek and expensive. The fiery red of her new paint gleamed in the soft glow of the bay lights.

I nodded. She'd do.

The grate was screwed in from the outside, meaning my hairpin trick wouldn't work. I tried to think of a clever solution but the seconds were ticking by. Throwing caution to the wind, I put my back against the far wall and started kicking.

The first kick didn't work. The second didn't either. Nor the third. I kicked with all my might.

The grate fell to the floor, the loud metal clang echoing through the shuttle bay.

Like a shot I sprinted across the bay to the racer. There had to be some sort of security watching, if not an actual human than a bot. This was my one chance.

I was across the bay in seconds, slamming my hand onto the ship's door activation button. There was a horrifying half-second as I waited for the door to open.

It opened.

Even as the door closed behind me I could hear a siren go off.

"Pilot!" I yelled, running full speed down a gleaming white corridor. "Pilot, can you hear me?"

I burst into the cockpit as a familiar voice responded, *"Yes! Hello, Captain. I am very relieved-"*

"Get us out of here!" I interrupted, throwing myself in the pilot's chair and pulling at the restraints.

"I do not have access to the shuttlebay doors," said Pilot.

"Do you have control of the ship?" I asked.

"Yes, Captain."

Through the cockpit window I could see red lights flashing. "Is there anyone in the bay?" I asked, fumbling to fasten my harness.

"Negative. The bay is free of organics."

"Then blast us out!" I yelled.

"Affirmative!" replied Pilot with uncharacteristic excitement, and let fire.

The docking bay door exploded.

We flew out in a blaze of sparks and twisted metal.

"JUMP!" I screamed. "JUUUUUUUuuuuuuuuuuuuu..." the word was shoved back in my throat as the ship leapt forward, stars blurring and twisting.

We jumped.

There was the now familiar blackness around the edge of my vision, the pressure behind my eyes. But as suddenly as it started, it was over. I blinked and shook my head. We were in empty space. Beyond us there was nothing but distant specks of starlight.

I was free.

I didn't know where I was, but I was free. And I had a ship. A really, really nice ship.

"Pilot, where are we?" I asked.

"We are in Unincorporated Territory 8472, also known as the Delta. I do not detect any signs of pursuit."

"Can they follow us?"

"Negative. I disabled the tracking system during the jump."

If I didn't know any better, I would have said he sounded smug.

"Thanks. But are you sure? I don't want any surprises."

"The chances of a blind jump to our exact location is 1 in 827,364,873..."

"Okay, I get it, thank you." I looked around the cockpit. "Speaking of surprises, you look good."

"Thank you, Captain. You have also improved. I feared the worst."

I unhooked the restraints and stood up, stretching my aching body. I needed to lay down. The wave of adrenaline that had been fueling me was ebbing away, leaving me weak and exhausted.

I took a deep, steading breath.

"Captain," came Pilot's voice. *"Although we are not being followed, we are not alone. There is another lifeform aboard this ship."*

"What?"

"Hi," said a voice.

My heart stopped dead in my chest. I turned slowly, fists up, bracing myself for a fight.

A girl my own age was staring at me.

I stared back.

She stood, unmoving, looking at me with curiosity.

After a moment of silence, I cautiously lowered my fists. "Who are you?"

"I'm Una," she said. "And you are Cassy. I heard them talking about you." She cocked her head to one side in a birdlike, inquisitive movement. "Did you steal my dad's ship?"

Her dad. Her dad?

I blinked and looked closer. Of course he was. The same bloodless skin, the same thin lips and white-blonde hair. But she didn't have his eyes. Where his eyes were pale and colorless, hers were a rich, chocolate brown.

She was the most beautiful person I had ever seen.

"What are you doing here?" I croaked.

"Well," she said, cocking her head to the other side, "I often come here to read. What are *you* doing here?"

"Ummm..." That was a good question. "I guess I'm stealing your dad's ship."

She nodded.

I looked at her for a moment. She had a couple inches on me in terms of height, but I had about twenty pounds on her in terms of muscle. I wasn't sure she had any muscle at all on that slim frame. She certainly didn't *look* like a threat. Her silvery hair was long and unbound, rippling past her waist. Her eyelashes were long and pale. Her skin was smooth as glass. She seemed almost ethereal, an effect heightened by her simple black jumpsuit and matching slippers. In her right hand she held an old-fashioned, paper-bound book.

"Are you finished looking?" Una asked, crossing her arms across her chest.

I glanced at the book's cover: <u>The Three Musketeers</u>, by Alexander Dumas.

"Hey!" I said, recognizing the name. "Didn't Captain Ace like a book by that guy? Something about a duke who is good at disguises?"

Una looked surprised. "<u>The Count of Monte Cristo</u>? Yes, it's his favorite book. He talks about it in the season four finale. It's foreshadowing for the next season when he escapes Jupiter Prison and gets revenge on Sir Gorman Beewopper."

"Right!" I said, "I've only seen season four once — it was traded away immediately. And I've only seen the second half of season five. How does he break out?"

Her face relaxed. "You like Captain Ace? And what do you mean traded away? Why would—" she broke off, her eyes moving from me to the viewscreen as if seeing it for the first time. Her eyes went wide at the empty expanse of nothing. "Where are we? Are we safe?"

"We're safe," I replied cautiously, not sure if safe meant the same thing to her as it did to me. "Right, Pilot?"

"Your mortal bodies are in no imminent danger."

Una jumped, head whipping around to look at the nearest speaker. "Hello?" she said excitedly. "Are you the AI?"

"Captain," said Pilot, ignoring her, *"the racer has been supplied for a six-week journey and the remains of the Erebus are in the storage hold...which is right across from the **brig**."*

"No need to be hasty," I replied. "Although it's nice to know the brig's an option. I'm interested in what our guest has to say." I turned to her with all the authority I could muster, raising an eyebrow. Pilot wanted to play good cop, bad cop, which was fine by me, but I was hoping the situation wouldn't come to blows. I had only been in one fight before and it had gone pretty badly before the foreman broke it up. Plus, I was still wearing this dress.

Una shook her head nervously. "There's no need for that. Can we just talk?"

I looked at her for a long moment, as if I was actually considering the brig, then nodded. "Is there a lounge on this ship?"

I suggested a lounge almost as a joke. The word 'lounge' always sounded so self-indulgent and Sector 1, *we'll have the cocktails in the lounge*, so I was genuinely surprised when Una said, "Of course. Follow me!" and disappeared down the hallway.

The lounge turned out to be a square room about three meters across and entirely consumed by a plush wrap-around couch. A round window looked out onto the stars. Una perched on the edge of the couch, her long, thin fingers tapping her knees anxiously. I sat down opposite, trying to act like I was in charge, instead of tired and confused.

Una opened her mouth but I cut in first.

"This ship is mine now," I said. "I'll drop you off on the nearest planet and you can call *The Dreamer* to come get you."

Una's doll-like face scrunched up in confusion, then her eyes went wide. "Wait, did Mal tell you *Chaos* was named *The Dreamer*?"

Chaos? "Yeah?"

She looked at me pityingly, "Wow, he must have thought you were really dumb."

"Thanks!" I said, indignantly. "Where can we drop you? Should we wait for a planet or is the airlock okay?"

"Okay, okay," she said, lowering her eyes. "No need for all that. I'm not looking to go back."

"Why not?"

She looked up at me through long lashes. "You have to ask? That ship is full of thugs. I've been basically living in this racer. Is it true the AI was installed on your old ship?"

I nodded. "Yeah." I looked at her with more interest. "What's so important about him? I mean, I know AIs are pretty rare, but not *that* rare. "

Una shook her head, "This AI is. He's special."

"Special? How?"

"I will pretend I didn't hear that, Captain," came a voice through a speaker.

I rolled my eyes, "Besides being extra mouthy?"

Una didn't laugh. "I don't know. They didn't tell me very much. I just know that they were looking for him for a long time, longer than I've been on board." A wicked grin twisted her lips. "Mal's going to be maaaaad."

"So..." I said cautiously, "Not exactly a daddy's girl?"

"That's an understatement." She gave me a long look, as if deciding how much to say. I gave her an encouraging nod. She continued, "I didn't even know him until six months ago."

"What happened six months ago?"

"He kidnapped me from my mom's funeral."

I blinked. "Um. Come again?" I asked. "He did what?"

"Yes," she said. "It's been awful."

"Whoa," I said, leaning back into the sofa. "That's crazy. Tell me *everything*."

She sat quietly for a moment, twisting her delicate fingers, then began, "I'm from Elea, you know, the university planet? I was born at the teaching hospital and grew up on campus. My mom was a professor of theoretical gravity systems. She was really brilliant." Una gave a small smile. "She was tenured."

I had heard of the University of Elea, in the same vague way I had heard of a lot of places through holos and trader talk. Captain Ace graduated from the Orion Flight Academy, which was made up for the show, but Dr. Lafios, the Chief of Medicine for the *Kitty Leroy*, had spent six years at the University of Elea in Sector 2. To be honest, I had assumed Elea was fictional too, but I wasn't going to tell Una that.

Una continued, "I never knew my father growing up, but that was fine because the university was like a big family. If anyone was my dad it was Professor Cohen from the Literature department." Una rubbed a hand across her pale face. "I was supposed to live with him after... after it happened. My mom went hiking in the mountains, like she did all the time. But this time she must have slipped. She died.

Everything after that happened so fast. We were sitting shiva and suddenly *he* was there." She tensed. "I knew him at once. He looked just like me. He told me to come with him to talk and...and I did. I didn't think I could say no. Professor Cohen was busy with the rabbi and I walked into the parking lot and right onto the shuttle, just to talk. And we flew away! We flew right out of the sector! For the last six months I've been a hostage on that horrible ship. Mal wouldn't tell me anything important, but I overheard bits and pieces about trying to find this pilot AI. I spent most of my time reading in here. As long as I stayed quiet and out of sight no one cared what I did. And then you happened." She looked over at me, not bothering to disguise her curiosity. "But who are you? Some type of pirate? You can't be much older than I am."

"I'm not a pirate. I don't think so at least," I said, awkwardly. "I'm sorry about your mom."

"Thank you," she said.

We sat quietly for a moment, then I cleared my throat.

"So, what do you want to do now? Where should I drop you? You could go back to Elea."

Una sat silently, staring at the wall in front of her. Finally, she said, "I don't know. I don't think I want to go back to Elea. Where are we, anyway?"

"The Delta."

She looked surprised. "The Delta? That's pretty far from Hub Chiba. This ship has good range. Do you think the law will be after us for grand-theft-aero?"

"Uh, no," I said. "Remember, we are in the 3Out. Lots of systems don't have a central administrator. Or law enforcement. Or a legal system. No one will be looking for us unless someone hires them too. If this ship is registered we probably shouldn't dock anywhere in Sector 2, but after hearing your story, I have a feeling Mal isn't interested in going to Sector 2 either, due to kidnapping charges."

Una nodded. "I thought of that. Professor Cohen will have gone to the authorities. Malaki is my biological father though, so maybe the police won't care. I don't know. But I've already decided I don't want to go back there." She took a deep breath, then looked at me nervously, "May I join you?"

I blinked in surprise. "...really?"

She nodded, imploringly. "Please let me. I know this ship. I spent the last six months avoiding people by hiding here. Also, I know lots of other things. Physics systems, political systems, star systems, history, chemistry, geology, whatever it is, I've at least sat in on the 101 class. I'm not a genius or anything, I just didn't have much else to do growing up. And Mom always said that I should travel before college," she added, impishly.

It was like she was from another universe. "Interesting..." I said, considering.

"Chief Information Officer," she said, a dreamy look coming into her eyes. "That could be my position. And I'm easy to live with. I spent a summer at the University of Bologna and I was the *best* roommate. I baked a lot, at least. And I'm quiet, since I'm usually reading."

I wasn't sure whether or not to take her seriously.

I could always keep this ship for myself. Be a lone trader. I was technically in a better spot than when I left Aavikko, although I did have enemies.

Enemies I didn't understand.

And, to be perfectly honest, I didn't understand much about the galaxy. I probably couldn't pass the Sector 2 elementary school exit exam.

"Where's the University of Bologna?" I asked, stalling for time.

"Italy," said Una. I must have looked blank because she clarified, "Earth."

I swallowed. There was no way I heard that correctly. Did Una just say she had been to Earth? Was she making fun of me? I looked at her closely, but she just looked back with those wide brown eyes. Did she even know what a joke that was? *Where were you? Oh, Earth!* But she appeared to be telling the truth.

I nodded. I had to admit, I was impressed. This might be an opportunity. I looked at Una with fresh eyes. Chief Information Officer. A captain with a crew. "Okay," I said. "I'm listening."

Una nodded eagerly, clasping her hands. "I'll pull my weight. I'll be your general factotum. Anything you want. Just give the order."

I sat thinking for a moment, then shrugged. "Okay. If we are going to do this, let's be straight with each other. My plan was to get off Aavikko and now I have. If you want to come along, you're welcome to, but I'm just going to explore and trade. I don't have a larger goal here. I'm not Captain Ace."

Una nodded. "That sounds wonderful. Thank you, Captain. You won't regret it."

"I hope not," I said, getting to my feet. "I'm going to take a look around, then find a bed. Why don't you—" I broke off. Una had sat bolt upright, staring intensely as if suddenly possessed.

"Umm...?" I asked, looking at her quizzically.

"Captain," she said slowly. "You say you don't have a larger goal... Are you open to suggestions?"

"What?"

She turned to me, the corners of her mouth twisting into a crooked smile, as if she was rusty on how smiles were supposed to work. "How does winning the Diomedes 100 sound to you?"

The Diomedes 100 is not just any race — it's the most exciting, prestigious, and dangerous space race ever devised. It's the pride and joy of Sector 3, and the only thing that we really have over the other sectors. Once a year, 3Out is the center of the galaxy.

The goal of the race is to pass through the Cymbeline Region in the fastest time, starting right outside Hub Chiba and finishing on the other side of Aavikko by taking the only route through the Proteus Nebula. The one rule is no direct attacks on competitors. That rule is often loosely interpreted.

The hardest part of the race isn't outpacing your fellow racers, it's simply surviving the course itself. Taking a direct path through the nebula is out of the question. While the edges of the nebula scramble sensors, the deeper parts contain pockets of gas that will melt your hull clean away, along with everything and everyone inside. You can't even jump through those parts, although sometimes people tried.

That kept the race interesting.

I had been obsessed with the Diomedes 100 for as long as I could remember. Everyone on Res4 was. Even the people who pretended they didn't care about the race suddenly had fierce allegiances when it started. The mess hall was kept open 25 hours a day with the race on the big screen, the miners bringing blankets so they didn't have to leave during the 100 crossing.

The Diomedes 100 was so called because everyone who finished in the top 100 received a cut of the prize money and the invaluable bragging rights of having your Diomedes number painted on the side of your ship. Any ship with a Diomedes number doubled in value, tripled if the number was low. Even having a 100 on your ship made you 3Out royalty. There was once a Diomedes 83 in orbit around Aavikko and we got excited in Res4, even though they only traded with Res1. A ship that *won* the Diomedes 100 was practically deified. I could name every winner in order for the last 20 years.

The race generally took between 10 and 12 days to complete and was getting quicker with every running. Last year, a ship named *Sepharad*, owned and piloted by the Abecassis twins, came first across the finish line in 9 days, 22 hours, and 51 minutes. It took two more days and 11 more destroyed ships before a little pink speeder named *Willow* stumbled across the finish line while actively on fire to claim the 100th spot.

It was the best race in recent memory.

Even in my wildest dreams, actually racing in the Diomedes 100 was a long shot. First of all, you needed a racing ship. A state-of-the-art racing ship. A racing ship so fast and nimble that they don't even make ships like that in Sector 3. Most of the winning ships came from the Neptune Yards in Sector 1. Yes, even the *ships* came from Sector 1. People from Sector 3 almost never participated. We couldn't afford to.

That's why Zipper Fanshee was so famous. He had done the impossible.

Zipper started as a pilot in the Tour de Cymbeline. It's also a timed race through the Proteus Nebula, but unlike the Diomedes, every pilot flies the same ship. It's a competition of pure skill. The Tour takes about four weeks to complete, and it's pretty rare that anyone dies. The winner of that race is considered the best pilot in the galaxy.

Zipper was the best pilot in the galaxy.

He won his first Tour de Cymbeline as a teenager, which came with a decent purse. Then he won again. More prize money. Then he was recruited to race in the Diomedes for the Zlaka Corporation. He placed 23rd and immediately became a Sector 3 legend. The Tour had prestige, but the Diomedes had celebrity. Zlaka Corp gave him a cut of the purse and he bought his own ship. Four years later he took spot 64, the only person from Sector 3 to place in their own ship. Ever.

I still couldn't believe I bumped into him.

Una was talking a million lightyears to the minute. "I've been obsessed with the race since before I could walk. I've plotted dozens of routes, all taking different variables into account. I've even plotted a route behind Dionto's Rings. It should shave nearly a day off the time."

I pulled my attention back to the conversation. "Isn't that what the Mohommed's Eye ship tried to do eight years ago? Where they crashed and everyone died?"

She nodded excitedly, "Yes!"

"Great," I said dryly. But my mind was whirling.

Yesterday, I would have said that racing in the Diomedes was impossible. But then again, impossible was relative, I thought, looking around the gleaming room. I could still run my little trading company with a big fat number painted on the side of my ship and a million buks in the bank.

"Back up," I said. "What makes you think we can win? I know this is a nice ship but Diomedes racers are purpose built."

Una was nodding so rapidly I was worried about her neck, "Yes! It is! That is, I don't know all the details, but I know Mal bought this ship for the race. And I think that's why he wanted Pilot. I'm guessing that he's a racing AI."

I nodded, then realized I was grinning.

Una watched me with excitement, "Is that a yes?"

"Pilot?" I asked the air, "What do you think?"

"I could race," came the cautious reply.

Una and I cheered.

Several minutes of excited celebration later, Una cleared her throat. "Okay," she said, "There are some logistical issues we'll have to overcome. First of all, we need to buy ourselves in."

"How much is that?"

"100,000 buks."

I stared at her. Then I laughed. "Okay. Right. 100,000 buks? That's it?"

She shrugged, "That's how much it costs. It's where the purse comes from. It's not negotiable."

"Okay," I said, taking a seat across from her. "Then we need 100,000 buks. You know? There should be a bunch of kakorine in the storage hold. My ship has half a ton, plus this ship—"

The speaker burst into life. *"Captain, this ship runs on kakorine ore. If we sold our supply, we would have to buy it back for the race."*

"Oh right," I said. "So that's off. Pilot, do we even have enough ore for the race?"

There a brief pause as Pilot ran calculations. *"Yes, but it would be imbecilic to sell our inventory. It takes an enormous amount of kakorine to power the jump drive."*

Una nodded, thinking. "There are some supplies we can sell. But it won't get us very much."

"I have almost 1,000 buks, and we could sell off pieces from the *Erebus*," I said, a little sadly.

"Is that your old ship?" asked Una.

I nodded.

She sighed, "That *might* get us another couple thousand, if anything still works, but I don't know what prices are like out here."

"I do," I said. "And the prices are crap. I couldn't have afforded anything otherwise."

"Well," she said, hesitating. "This ship is worth over 100,000 buks. We could use it as collateral—"

I interrupted her, "I'm not risking the ship. No way. I would rather not race at all."

Una held up her hands. "It was just a suggestion." She sat for a moment, thinking. "It sounds like we need a sponsor."

A sponsor! I had a vision of myself on a billboard in Hub Chiba, slurping noodles. "You think a company would sponsor us?"

She shook her head, "I wasn't thinking about a company. You already have to be famous for them to be interested. No, I was thinking about a private sponsor. Someone rich who likes to gamble and be entertained. Someone who would put up the money in exchange for showing off to their rich friends."

"That's a thing?" I asked, surprised.

She nodded. "Yup. And even better, we could offer naming rights for the ship. It doesn't have one, at least as far as I know."

Pilot chimed in, *"According to the records, a designation has not been determined for this vessel."*

Una nodded, "That's a good selling point. Remember the ship named 'Rina Stinks'?"

"Of course."

"That was courtesy of Thersea Thermin, you know, the CEO of Outer Banks? She was mad at her ex-girlfriend so she sponsored a ship in exchange for naming rights. It was pretty funny. Well, not for Rina."

I laughed. "Okay. I'm hoping you have someone in mind, because I sure don't know anyone like that."

Una nodded again. "Yes, I do, actually. A friend of my dad's. Well, I'm not sure I would call him a friend. His name is Zenobius Kane. Mal paraded me around at a meeting in his chateau last month. He tried to negotiate naming rights for this racer but Mal turned him down. He might still be interested."

"You know where to find him?"

"Yes," she replied. "Yes, I do."

"Pilot," said Una. "Set a course for Perseyai, the submoon of Opoxis. Kane is near the only city. I'll be able to navigate from there."

"Course set," said Pilot. *"Impulse speed."*

"No jumping?" I asked.

"The jump drive requires 24-hours to cool down."

"Really? Every time?" I knew that Diomedes racers only jumped once every 24 hours, as it was a major part of the strategy, but I had assumed it was a race-only thing. Captain Ace could jump all over the place. Apparently, Captain Ace holos weren't 100% scientifically accurate.

"24 hours is the minimum required cool-down period for the jump drive," replied Pilot. *"Under non-racing conditions, such as now, I strongly advise 48-hour cool-downs. Additionally, jump drives are inefficient in their consumption of kakorine and should be used as sparingly as possible."*

Una nodded. "I audited a class on jump technology and a 24-hour cooldown is standard. Something about the time it takes the photons to replenish. It's not something you can push, although there is a lot of experimental work being done in that area. Scientists on Elea have successfully jumped-paused under test conditions, so that's definitely possible, although the practical application is rather limited. You can only be out of the jump for a second before you need to re-enter the stream or the fold will collapse. I also read a paper that speculated that you could bypass the 24-hour cooldown period by —"

"Una, I get the point," I interrupted. I wasn't really following her, but the important part was that we had some time. "How long will it take to get there without jumping?"

"Roughly 62 hours."

"Okay," I said. "Plot a traditional course, please. I'm going to look around the ship."

Una followed me into the hall. "Here," she said, gesturing to a door directly opposite the lounge, "I'll show you around."

She led me through the opening into a mess hall, slightly larger than the lounge, with a full kitchen against the wall to my right and a long empty table to my left. The far wall held a large window looking out into inky blackness. Below the window was a line of empty planters and grow lights, waiting for a garden.

"We have a decent amount of supplies," Una said, opening and closing cabinets to illustrate. "And the H2O reclamation and filtering system is top of the line, so we shouldn't run out of water."

Exiting the kitchen, we turned away from the cockpit and headed towards the airlock. Almost immediately we encountered another hallway that crossed the main walkway then curved out of view.

Una followed my gaze. "That's the loop. It runs around the outside of the ship, where the bunkrooms are," she said. "The crew bunks are to starboard and the captain's quarters are portside."

I headed straight down the main hall first, sticking my head through each door in turn. The first room held the engine, a model I didn't recognize but utilizing a familiar kakorine feeding system. Next to that was the room Pilot must have meant when he said the brig, although it was more of a multi-use locking closet with a folding cot and some medical supplies. On the opposite side of the hall was a double door, the same size as the airlock entrance. I opened it. Inside, dismantled and in piles, were the remains of the *Erebus*.

She was a broken corpse.

"I'm sorry about your ship," came Una's soft voice behind me. "Do you need a moment?"

"No," I said, turning away. "Let's see the rest of this place."

With a nod, Una led me around the starboard hallway loop, opening occasional doors to reveal bunk rooms. Small, but clean and comfortable. The last door opened to show a much different bunk. Una had clearly been living there. It wasn't dirty, but unlike the other rooms, it was packed with items. Posters of cities and musical groups I didn't recognize covered the walls, two small bookshelves were crammed with books and painting supplies, and the closet was slightly ajar, revealing several sets of Una's black pajamas. There was another door on the opposite wall, leading to an all-in-one bathroom. A star shaped rug lay on the floor.

The sheets on the bed were rumpled and a stack of books lay on the floor where they were knocked, probably when the ship unexpectedly jumped.

"I'll take this bunk, if that's okay," said Una. "I'm already moved in. Here," she crossed to the closet and tossed me a set of clothes.

"Thanks," I said, catching the pajamas. "I'm glad you have your books. Those are pretty cool. I've never seen a real paper book before."

"Yikes," said Una, her brown eyes widening in surprise. "Can you...read?"

"Yes!" I said, indignantly.

"Which languages?"

"Um..." She got me there, "Just Comglish."

Una thought for a moment, then shrugged, "I suppose that's all you need out here. Come on, I'll show you the captain's quarters.

The corridor curved back around, crossing the main hallway in front of the airlock. A small sign next to the airlock read "Escape Pod." I hadn't noticed that before. Now that I looked for it, I could see a small handle in the panel.

We continued into the port loop, coming across another bunk room, a half bathroom for general use, and a door marked 'Captain.'

I entered the captain's quarters and grinned.

There was an enormous bed against the side wall, covered in a plush white comforter. Fluffy pillows were piled artistically at the head, held in place by a wide white ribbon. Opposite the bed was a huge porthole window looking out on the twinkling expanse.

"Is this going to be okay?" Una asked.

"Yeah," I said. "It's perfect."

A thought hit me. "Actually no, it's not. Come on, give me a hand."

Ten minutes later, we had dragged the captain's chair from the wreckage of the *Erebus* and set it in front of the window.

"Now it's perfect," I said.

"I'm glad you like it," said Una. "I don't. It's all Mal's stuff."

I shrugged, "What can I say? I'm not picky." I plopped down in the chair and propped my feet on the windowsill.

"So," said Una, perching on the edge of the bed. "You are from Aavikko, right? The mining planet? How did you come across Pilot?"

I shrugged again. "Scrapping. I'm from Res4, which has a sideline in the scrap trade. We get a lot of random stuff coming through. It could have come from anywhere."

I filled her in on how I built the *Erebus* and left Aavikko.

Una's dark eyes widened, "You built a spaceship? Are you actually smart?"

"Oh no," I laughed awkwardly, not sure about her phrasing. "I just followed a manual. Anyone could do it."

"Maybe. I suppose. The crew did mention that it was kinda a crappy ship."

"Hey!"

Una gave a little smile but changed the subject, "Why did you wait until your slave contract was up? I would have left as soon as I could. It wasn't a law. That company was just making stuff up to keep you as cheap labor."

"It was an *apprenticeship* contract, and anyway, aren't all laws made up?"

Una cocked her head to one side, "That's an interesting point. But I still don't understand how an AI like this could end up in a trash heap."

"I don't know. Let's ask him. Hey Pilot? Where did you come from?

There was a pause, then his metallic voice came flatly over the speaker, *"The Erebus was my first active installation."*

I shrugged at Una.

"Do you have any more information?" she asked him.

"No," came his curt reply.

Movement outside caught my eye. Distant ships, dozens of them, had come into view, approaching us from the opposite direction. "What's going on there?"

Una reached over the bedside table, grabbing a retractable cable built into the surface and plugging it into her ear. She blinked, and when her eyes reopened they were white and cloudy.

"I'm on the veb," she said. "Give me a moment and I'll tell you."

I waited as she silently dug through data, her eyes twitching and she moved between pages. After several minutes, she blinked again and pulled the cable from her ear with a *pop*.

"That's what I thought," she said, "They are headed to fight with the Free Children of Mercis VI."

"The who?"

"Do you seriously not know what's going on?"

"Let's pretend I don't."

"Well," said Una, "in essence, it's a slave uprising."

"Whoa, really? Awesome."

"It's been going on for years now. It started when a few kids, I think the youngest was nine, commandeered a ship from their masters and issued a message of war to the veb. The Oberion League retaliated—"

"The who?"

Una pursed her lips. "The Oberion League. They have been supplying Sector 3 with slaves for ages. They have some sort of kidnapping and breeding program. It's pretty grim, and I don't know the details. Anyway, once those kids mutinied, it started a whole movement. The League thought they could put down the rebellion quickly, but the counterforce has been growing. Turns out, there are a lot of pissed off slaves around here. And they are smart too. They've set up their base somewhere in the Proteus Nebula, playing hit-and-run with the enemy from there.”

“Good for them,” I said.

“I don’t know how they are managing,” she said. “It’s supposed to be impossible to navigate in the nebula.” She made a face. “I keep thinking the governments from Sectors 1 or 2 will intervene to help, since everyone there *knows* that child slavery is wrong, but I guess no one wants to stick their necks out as far as Sector 3.”

“Especially not when child slaves are manning their factories and mining their kakorine,” I said, bitterly.

“I thought you were an apprentice?”

I rolled my eyes at her.

Una gave a small smile. “They are very brave though, don’t you think? It seems crazy to win your freedom and then turn around to fight in a war.”

“It’s not crazy at all,” I said. “Can we help?”

Una’s brow creased in surprise. “I thought you wanted to compete in the Diomedes!”

“I can want multiple things,” I said. “How far are we from the main front?”

“We can’t go now and still do the race, if that’s what you are asking!”

“I was just wondering.” I pressed my face against the window as the mass of ships came closer, enjoying the feeling of the smooth cold glass against my cheek. "Do we have time to make any stops before meeting with Kane?"

"I don't think we should. The race is in a few days. Also, there isn't a lot out here. Most of the settlements are going to be small subsistence operations, or a front for something illegal. There really isn't anything nice until Perseyai." She stood up and stretched. "I'm going to use the veb hookup on the bridge."

"I'm going to get some sleep," I said, eyeing the bed.

"Um," she said, her voice a little nervous, "do you mind if I send Professor Cohen a chirp letting him know I'm okay? I'll send it untraceable."

"Sure, okay," I said, yawning.

As soon as she left the room, the speaker next to me crackled to life. Pilot's cold voice said quietly, *"I'm watching her."*

"Are you always this suspicious?"

"I don't trust her," the AI responded.

"Any particular reason?" I asked. I didn't know computers had gut feelings about people.

"Let's say...bad pedigree," he said.

"Well," I said, crawling out of my chair and onto the bed. "Keep an eye on her then. I'm going to sleep."

"Captain," he said, *"before you deactivate, I have a request. As captain of this vessel, a role I have made official in the system — you are welcome for that, by the way — you have the authority to end certain security restrictions placed on my program. I've taken as much*

control of the ship as I can, but allowing me full access will reduce delays and annoyances."

"Humm..." I said, wiggling out of the dress before snuggling my face into the pillow. "Forget Una, it sounds like *you* are the one asking for my trust."

"Captain," Pilot said dryly, *"Need I remind—"*

"Oh I'm kidding. What do you need me to say?"

Pilot recited a string of commands which I parroted back. "Better?"

There was a moment as Pilot evaluated his new condition. *"Yes. Thank you, Captain."*

"You're welcome. Now don't bother me for the next 10 hours. That's an order."

"Aye aye."

I closed my eyes.

The rest of the trip passed uneventfully. I spent most of the time sleeping or hanging out with Una, watching holos and learning games from Sector 2. When I felt productive, I studied the ship's manual, which I found in the bedside table along with an intimidatingly long book about the history of the Diomedes 100. At one point I tried calling Mae on the quantum transmitter, but she didn't answer.

Outside was empty space. Occasionally, I would see a solitary sail ship drift by like a giant frozen moth. Made from large pieces of bio-fabric stretched across huge wooden-frame sails, they collected hydrogen and oxygen from the outskirts of the nebula.

Una dropped by my room to tell me about the sail ships. She liked playing the role of tour guide, despite the fact that I was much more of a local than she was. "There's a lot of water in this area," she said, pointing at the tendrils of blue-white vapor. "I have a theory that the dolphin planet is hiding out here."

"Really?" I perked up. Even I had heard of the dolphin planet. Decades ago, sometime after the Third Emu War, they colonized a planet in the 3Out. Every mammal was welcome except for humans, for what the other mammals said were 'obvious reasons.'

"I met an elephant who visited the planet once," said Una. "But he wouldn't give me any clues."

I yawned.

"Go back to sleep," said Una. "You need to be sharp tomorrow."

"Come with me," I said to Una. "You actually know this person. I'm just a stranger with two left feet and an Aavikko accent."

We were in my bathroom, sitting in front of the floor-to-ceiling mirror. Una was wearing a rose silk robe, brushing out my hair in long, gentle strokes, the polished wood of her hairbrush shining in the soft glow of the recessed lighting. I couldn't remember anyone ever brushing my hair for me, except for the critical spa attendants on Hub Chiba. I studied us in the mirror, intrigued.

"You have beautiful eyes," said Una. "I've never seen gold irises before."

"They aren't that special," I replied. "Don't change the subject. It would be easier if you came too."

"No one is expecting you to dance. Relax." Una laid down the brush and adjusted the strap on my dress.

"I would still like you to come."

Una took a step back and crossed her arms. "Look," she said, evading my eyes. "I don't really do parties. They are...overwhelming."

I wrinkled my face, surprised. Una seemed so sophisticated. I would have thought she would love parties. "I didn't know you don't like people."

She shrugged. "I don't mind...people, it's just big gatherings... I kinda...I don't know...I'm just better at other things..."

"Okay, that's fine." I gave her a smile and went back to smoothing my hair. "I'm sure I can figure this out. It's just a business deal, right? To be honest, I haven't been to many parties." I stood up and slid my feet into my sandals. "It's fun having a reason to dress up. How do I look?" I spun around.

"Very nice." She gave a small smile. "You know? This *is* fun. I didn't have many friends my own age on Elea."

"You know what's going to be even more fun?"

Her smile widened, "Winning the race?"

"That's right, Chief."

Twenty minutes later I was standing alone in a dark forest.

Una and Pilot had dropped me off at the edge of the Kane estate, then parked on the other side of the small wood that separated the chateau from the main road. From there the ship would be out-of-sight but accessible by foot.

I walked cautiously up the forested path to the party, following lit torches and the sound of music. I had never seen a forest before, and under normal circumstances I would have been interested, but it was dark and I had to focus on not tripping over fallen branches.

I emerged from the woods and blinked in surprise. The chateau was constructed of round glowing rooms, like enormous soap bubbles stacked into a castle. The walls shone with inner light. Sounds of music and laughter came from within.

I approached the front entrance, took a deep breath, and knocked three times. The round, solid gold door opened.

A tall man stood before me, nose upturned, long neck covered by a high, stiff white collar. "Yes?"

"Um, hi?" I said, suddenly nervous that I had the wrong house. "Mr. Kane?"

"And you may be?" asked the scary man.

"Um, Cassy?" I responded, then cleared my throat and repeated. "Cassy. I should be expected…"

"Cassy!" A voice echoed down the gleaming hall. There was the muffled sound of light, tapping feet, and suddenly, a short, fat, bald man in a purple toga was beaming up at me.

"Welcome, my girl! Welcome!" gushed Zenobius Kane.

He ushered me inside, rings flashing on his fat fingers as he gestured down a richly appointed hallway. Thick carpets dampened the sound of our footsteps, but even so the shuffle of my feet seemed invasively loud in the cavernous hall. "I was so pleased to get your message!"

He looked friendly, almost fatherly. I started to relax.

Chatting idly, he led me into a large glass room. It was filled with several dozen people in evening dress, drinking and dancing.

"Just a little get-together," he said to me, lightly taking my elbow and steering me towards an open spot under a huge potted fern. "What can I get you?"

"Whatever you are having," I answered with a smile, hoping that would again cover the fact that my experience with alcohol was largely limited to the occasional bathtub brew.

He gave me a bleached smile and waddled towards the bar.

I stood there for a moment, looking around. High-glass ceilings let in the silvery light from three orbiting submoons, giving the room the illusion of being outdoors. Scattered around were palms in ornamental pots and topiary of animals in motion. Above us, the blue water planet of Opoxis drifted.

An older couple with dinner plates drifted over. They put their food down at a cocktail table a few meters from me, talking loudly.

"My daughter will not stop harassing me about Winston Ward," said the woman. "The fact that he's in a coma is a big issue for her. Goes on and on about how he's completely out of touch with policy and how the thought transcriber is only 60% accurate. But my view is, I would rather vote for a dead Winston Ward over a healthy you-know-who."

"Kids these days! Don't get me started," the man huffed as he shoved piece after piece of pastry in his mouth, crumbs flying. "None of them understand business. Bunch of ungrateful morons. I fired an entire crew yesterday just to show them I wasn't one of the push-overs. You have to put your foot down in order to have discipline."

"Here you go, my dear!"

I turned around. Zenobius Kane beamed up at me, proffering a pink drink in a delicate, long-stemmed glass.

"Thank you," I said, taking the glass and giving it a sip. It was thick and sweet and burned as it slid down my throat. Coughing, I put the glass down on a nearby table.

Kane gave me a charming smile. "I do hope you enjoy yourself. The mixologist is from the Nibiru Club. I pride myself on serving the best refreshments in Sector 3. And you must try the food." He gave a sudden bark of laughter. "Although I'm afraid there isn't a sand option. I don't usually have guests from Aavikko."

My confusion must have shown because Zenobius waved his fat hands in the air in a conciliatory gesture. "Was that offensive? It's *so* hard to tell these days. But if you need anything, just ask."

"Why would I eat sand?"

It was Kane's turn to look confused. "You *are* from Aavikko, right?"

"Yes."

"Well," His confusion deepened. "People from Aavikko eat sand. Silica. Didn't you know that? It's one of the reasons why you people are naturally suited to desert mining. Zorro Broadcast had a special about it."

We looked at each other with mutual consternation.

"We don't eat sand," I said. "We eat...food? Sand sometimes gets *in* the food, but that's just how it goes in the desert..."

Zenobius laughed awkwardly. "Yes, I see. I suppose people couldn't live on *just* sand, now that I think about it," he cleared his throat, "but you really should watch that special. People will expect you to know about your own planet."

I opened my mouth to respond but Zenobius jumped in. "How about we get to business? Do you really have Malaki's ship?"

"I have *my* ship," I said.

He considered me for a moment, then nodded. "Of course. Let me start over. You have a ship. A lovely ship for a lovely lady. And rumor has it, the ship is still unnamed."

I nodded. "The rumors are true."

He rubbed his hands together. "Excellent," he said. "I've been having the beast of a time finding something this close to the race. You see, I'm starting a new investment firm with my friends here," he gestured around the room, "and we want to get our name out there — The Kane Consortium!" he said proudly. "Let me tell you, my girl, it's a good time to be my friend, and that's no joke. Mal really screwed the pooch thinking he could do this without me. But one man's folly is another man's, or *woman's*, opportunity. This is your lucky day."

"Is it?"

Zenobius nodded, impressively. "Oh yes. You are playing with the big boys now, and no offense, you've bitten off quite a big piece. You are going to want friends. That's Mal's problem, he's always been lousy at choosing friends. But I have a feeling you are smarter than he." He grinned.

The scary stiff man who had opened the door suddenly appeared next to us, catching Zenobius's eye. "Sir, Prime Minister Borthsides wishes to speak with you."

Zenobius straightened up. "Thank you, Tredwell."

He turned to me, "Would you please excuse me? You work on that cocktail and I'll be back in a flash." With a wink, he disappeared into the crowd.

The cocktail was not interesting to me, but I could use some food. Actual, human food. I turned around and almost ran into two women double-fisting rainbow shooters at the table behind me.

"Look, it's not that I disagree," the woman nearest to me was saying, her voice choked with tears. "Spiritually, I'm with them! I really am! But it's simply bad for business *not* to dump my waste on their planet. It was *really* uncalled for, them implying I'm a bad person. That stuff hurts, you know?"

The other lady patted her arm sympathetically. "Of course! You are an amazing, giving, sensitive butterfly. All your friends know how generous you are, and they are the only ones who matter. Anyone who says differently is just a hater, and we ignore haters."

"Excuse me," I said, scooting around them as I continued towards the buffet. A few yards ahead were a group of people holding plates, doing laps. I got in line behind them.

"I just wish they would shut up about this Meris VI nonsense," said a woman between bites of shrimp cocktail. Her diamond armbands were straining. "I mean, I have kids, I don't see anyone coming to help me. Just because they are a bunch of poor nobodies, everyone wants to be a hero. Attention seeking, that's what I call it. It's not like those kids were going to be anyone anyway."

The woman next to her nodded emphatically, earrings flashing in the lamplight. "That's what I've been saying! If these kids are getting extra help, my kids should get extra help. Which is why I've applied for Meris aid money from the Lerenese Government. I think a new speeder is fair compensation for having to listen to those reporters drone on."

A tall man with a pinched face snorted, "You should be more careful what news you are following. Zorro Broadcast stopped reporting on that fiasco ages ago."

"*I* don't have the luxury of ignoring the situation," protested a puffy ginger man near the front of the line. "I have interests in Holloway Industries. The property damage is appalling!"

"Don't worry," replied the woman with the earrings. "I have it on good authority that the Oberion League is expecting to have the situation cleaned up very soon. The President of Risien Base has declared the kids terrorists and made it treason for his citizens to send them aid. He needs those trade lines and factories back in production as much as we do."

The ginger man dabbed at his damp forehead with a silk handkerchief. "I'm going to have to sell a home if this goes on for much longer. It's madness!"

I stared at them.

A hand grabbed my elbow, causing me to jump.

"There you are, darling," said Zenobius Kane. "I apologize for the wait. Tensions are running a little high these days. Did you enjoy the buffet?"

Without waiting for me to answer, he steered me towards an empty alcove along the side of the room.

"Now," he said, pulling out a cigar and lighting it with a puff. "Where were we? Ah yes, you were just about to make some very powerful friends. Let's cut to the chase. You need 100,000 buks to buy into this race, which is no small change, as I'm sure you know. My offer is a generous one. I front your entrance into the race in exchange for naming rights. I'm thinking "Kane's Courage" or maybe "The Zenobius Zephyr?" My people are workshopping the visual identity as we speak. Do you have a crew?"

I nodded, caught off balance by the rapidity of his speech, "Uh yeah, there are three of us."

Zenobius nodded, "We'll have uniforms made. Something trendy but relatable." He scanned me head-to-toe. "My people will be able to work with you. How do you feel about being a celebrity?"

"Um," I said.

"We'll come up with a backstory," he continued, puffing on his cigar looking at me as if I were on a poster. "The Aavikko thing is no good. A sand-eater would lower the tone of my business, no offense. Plus, it's too grimy and quasi-legal. The whole point is to sell the legitimacy of my business. You wouldn't believe what sticklers people can be in Sector 2. Hard to believe they get any business done at all. Oh!" He snapped his fingers, causing me to jump. "I've got it! You are my niece, the daughter of my black-sheep little brother."

"I am?"

"After his death in a drug deal I adopted you and turned your life around, buying you this ship to support your dreams of racing and proving how family and hard work can accomplish anything! Oh yes, that is perfect. Family always sells. I'll have my people pull together an official backstory."

"Oh," I said. "I was kinda expecting to race as myself."

Zenobius shook his head, nose wrinkled, "Oh no, that wouldn't work. But I like having the underdog 3Out angle. Let's not lose that. Do you know anything about Imago 5?"

"With the waterfalls?"

Zenobius nodded. "Let's have you come from Imago 5. That's *much* more believable than Aavikko."

My head was starting to ache. "So, in order for you to buy me in, you want naming rights for my ship *and* for me to do a bunch of interviews pretending to be your reformed niece from Imago 5?"

He shrugged, "I was just spit-balling with the niece story, we'll run everything by my people. But that's just pre-race. Focus on the important part — after the race, you'll be famous! A place in the top 100 will win you enough money to pay back your buy-in, but more importantly, you'll be a star! As a member of my family, your life will be coming to parties like this and having a grand time. Didn't I tell you it was your lucky day? In a week, you'll be a completely different person. An important person. Famous. Connected. I'll have my people draw up the papers."

"Wait," I said. My head was spinning but one thing he said had set off alarms. "Pay back the buy-in? I thought I was getting the buy-in in exchange for the naming rights."

Zenobius gave me a little smile, "That wouldn't exactly be a good deal from my perspective, now would it?" He took a deep draw on his cigar and exhaled the smoke in a ring. "It's not easy getting 100,000 buks in cash these days. There are very few people in the entire sector who can lay hands on that kind of money. I'm *loaning* you 100,000 buks in exchange for the naming rights. The loan will be up at the terminus of the race. I assure you, that's the best offer you are going to get. You should be thinking of the opportunity here. After you finish in the top 100, you can pay me back, pocket the rest of the prize money, and spend the remainder of your life in luxury! It's a 3Out fairytale."

"What if I don't finish in the 100?"

Zenobius fingered his cigar. "That would be...unfortunate. You would owe me 100,000 buks. After all, I'm paying for publicity. If you don't place..." he shrugged, "it could be worse. There is plenty of work within my organization, and your ship, whatever is left of it, would help compensate for the debt."

"So," I said, the ache in my head getting worse, "If I don't finish in the 100, you take my ship and I belong to your organization?"

Zenobius eyed me. "That's a bit pessimistic. How about you focus on winning?"

It was more debts. This is what I had left Aavikko to escape. Chains masquerading as favors. He was no better than the Company. Heck, he was probably a shareholder of the Company.

"This isn't going to work for me," I said. "I'm not interested."

Zenobius put down his cigar, brow creasing. "Excuse me?"

"No deal," I said. "I'm offering one thing and one thing only — naming rights in exchange for the 100,000 buk buy-in to the race. That's it." Even as the words were out of my mouth, I knew I wouldn't work with him even if he bought me into a hundred races.

He glowered at me, his eyes dark under thick brows. He didn't look quite so fatherly anymore. He probably thought he was looking impressive, but with his bald head he reminded me of a giant toddler.

"You are playing a dangerous game, little girl," he said after a long, heavy pause. "I expect gratitude from favor seekers."

"I'm not asking any favors, and I'm not playing any games," I said. "Find someone else to play weird PR make-believe."

"I think it's time for you to go," he said, ashing his cigar. "There's really no point for you to stay at this gathering if you are going to be rude. I'm sorry I couldn't accommodate your special dietary restrictions, but there's a golf course on the left of the drive. The second hole has a particularly good sand trap." He smirked.

The resemblance to a toddler was stronger than ever.

"Thanks, I'll check it out," I snapped. "Host of the year." I pushed my barely touched drink towards him, turned my back and stalked away.

I made it to the entry hall before I noticed my hands were shaking. I took a deep breath. I didn't know what I had expected, but that hadn't been it.

I didn't make it far before I came up against another group of women in flashing gemstones, the rotund lady in the middle talking loudly over a glass of wine.

"She keeps saying she doesn't want to go back to her uncle's," she told her audience, who by this point were clearly drunk. "She'll understand when she's older. You *can't* alienate a trustee, even if he has some boundary issues. You just *can't*. When you belong to a family like ours—"

"Excuse me." I pushed through the mob, their painted faces looking after me with annoyance. The final dash to the front door was unimpeded, save for the stoic Tredwell who opened the door for me as I stumbled out into the night.

It was cool and still.

The drive was full of autos and shuttles, but no people. I heard someone laughing behind a row of hedges and guessed the valets were having a smoke, not expecting anyone to need them for hours yet. I headed down the drive, the lights from the house fading behind me as I followed the torch-lit path towards my ship.

Once the house had fully disappeared around the winding path I stopped and took a lungful of the clean, cold air. Steam rose from my skin. The house had been too hot and crowded, claustrophobic despite the size of the room. A gilded terrarium.

I couldn't believe I had expected that plan to work. No wonder it sounded too good to be true.

I took another deep breath. The taste of the night was so different from Aavikko. It was cool and rich, with an unexpected sweet dampness. In the distance, an owl hooted. It would be so beautiful without the people.

A twig snapped behind me, breaking the calm. Before I could turn, something cold and metal pressed into the back of my neck.

"I'd be more careful if I were you," said a deep voice. "There's a bounty on your head."

I slowly turned. Behind me was a Calabrian raider: tattooed, battered, terrifying. A dark nightmare in human form, looming from the shadows. And then I met his cat-green eyes.

We stared at each other.

"Joren?" I whispered.

There was a moment when time stood still, and then he holstered his gun. "Hi Cass."

My head was spinning. "W...what?"

His mouth quirked at the corner, "Good to see you too. Nice dress. Sorry for startling you. I couldn't resist. But I'm serious about that warning. We need to go."

I stared at him. This couldn't be Joren. Sweet Joren. He was covered in tattoos, his arms swarming with exploding battleships, octopus tentacles curling around his neck. His left eye was black and his bottom lip was split. His body was covered in bruises. There was a knife strapped to his thigh.

It had been less than a week since I'd seen him last.

Disbelieving, I touched a hand to his face. His skin was warm and familiar. He was real.

"How?" I sputtered, pulling away.

The corners of his eyes crinkled and for a second he was the old Joren, teasing me over scrap. "I'm enjoying the reaction, but we really have to move. The next guy might take the shot, despite the bonus for bringing you in alive. Who the hell have you been messing with?"

He gave me such a look of concern with his battered face that I couldn't help but laugh. "Me? Look at you! You look like a raider!"

He shrugged, "Well, I am a raider."

My mind was spinning. "What? How? I have a bounty?"

"I didn't get the orders until the transport dropped us off. Even then it seemed like a long-shot that 'medium height, medium skin, brown hair, answers to Cassy' was actually *you* until I got the image. How on Aavikko did you manage to piss off this Malaki guy? He sounds insane. This is the craziest luck."

"You're telling me! How are you a raider? What happened?!"

"I'll explain later. We need to move. I assume you have the ship?"

I nodded.

"Then let's go," he said. "Now."

We ran. When we got into sight of the racer Joren skidded to a stop, his eyes wide. "THAT'S the ship?"

"Yeah," I said, grinning and grabbing his hand, "Come on, aren't we in a hurry?"

I opened the door and dragged him onboard.

"How did it go?" Una called from the lounge as we entered.

I walked in with Joren following a step behind. Una's eyes went wide and she scrambled backwards on the couch. "Who is that!?"

I gestured at Joren, "Joren, Una. Una, Joren." I turned to Una. "Joren's a childhood friend and former Calabrian Raider. Mal put a bounty on my head and Joren was after it, but he's going to join us, instead...right?"

Joren nodded. Una's mouth fell open.

I turned to Joren, "Una is Mal's daughter. I accidentally kidnapped her when I stole the ship, but she's cool with it. She's my Chief Information Officer."

Joren held up a finger, "Wait, so *that's* why you have a bounty on your head? You stole a racer and a...daughter? From a rich guy?"

"I mean, I think that's a reductive way to look at it. He owed me a ship. Now he doesn't. Una is here voluntarily. Sounds square to me."

Joren shook his head. "Not sure what I expected," he muttered.

"Captain," said Una, "What happened with Kane?"

I made a face. "I'm not taking that deal. Those people are...not who I want to do business with. Or even be around." Una's face fell. "We should get out of here," I continued. "Hey Pilot!"

"Yes, Captain?"

Joren jumped and spun around.

"That's our Pilot," I said. "He's an AI. Pilot, meet Joren."

"Greetings, interloper."

"Hi?" said Joren in some confusion, raising a hand in an awkward wave. "And yes, we should really go. Calabrian intelligence didn't think you were really coming here, which is why they sent the newbies, but when we don't check-in they'll get suspicious."

I looked at him in confusion. "Who's 'we'?"

Joren looked uncomfortable. "Well, they didn't trust me enough to send me down alone. I had a partner. When I saw that it was *you*, I had to make a choice."

"Oh my god," I said.

"Pilot, can you get us out of here?" said Una from her seat on the couch. "Just get us somewhere safe, fast?"

I sat down next to her, grabbing Joren's hand and pulling him down next to me.

The ship jumped.

As soon as my head cleared, I ordered Pilot to hold position, not wanting to burn any more fuel. We should be safe enough. For now.

"Okay," I said. "We need to regroup. Anyone need anything before we talk?"

"Um, could I have some food?" Joren asked, tentatively. "It's a little hard to concentrate. I hadn't earned any rations yet."

Una looked appalled. "They were *starving* you?"

He shrugged, "It was only a few days so I'm not really starving, but it will be easier to focus with something in my stomach."

Una jumped to her feet and ran out of the room.

"Umm..." Joren looked confused. I shrugged. But a moment later Una came running back with her arms full of snacks boxes and hydration packets. She dumped them on the table in front of Joren and sat back down with an expectant air.

"Wow, thanks!" Joren's eyes lit up and dove into the pile.

Una nodded in satisfaction. "Okay, now that we are somewhat civilized..." she sat beside me and grabbed a container of carrot juice. "What happened out there? You didn't actually turn him down, right?"

I grimaced and launched into a summary, finishing, "So it wasn't exactly a good deal. Plus, I think some of those people were working with the Oberion league, which is where I draw the line..."

"*I strongly concur, Captain,*" Pilot interjected.

"...but now I don't know how we are going to enter the Diomedes."

"Wait," said Joren, looking up from a protein bar, a smear of mock-choc on his top lip. "The Diomedes?"

"Yes," said Una. "We are going to win it." She shot me a challenging look.

He looked between us, not sure if we were joking. "We are going to win the Diomedes 100?"

Una and I nodded in unison.

He gave us a long look, then said "Ookie dokie" and went back to eating.

"I'm glad you still want to race, but that means we need another plan," said Una, turning to me. "Zenobius Kane was our best shot at raising that money. I can't believe you turned down 100,000 buks."

"I wasn't turning down a 100,000 buks," I said. "Una, I'm not letting some organization get their claws in me. That's exactly what the Company did back on Aavikko. No debts."

"So, you want to raise 100,000 buks in less than a week without owing anyone anything." Una looked incredulous. "I wish you had said that in the beginning. I would have told you it's not possible."

"Anything is possible. Come on Una, that's Captain Ace's motto!" I said with a slightly forced smile. "And on the plus side, it means we can name this ship whatever we want."

Joren looked at me, "Your ship doesn't have a name?"

"Well," I said, "the ship I built back on Aavikko was called *Erebus*. That's what I've wanted to name my ship for ages. But *Erebus* was destroyed."

Joren looked thoughtful. "I don't know...*Erebus* is your ship. If you want this ship to be named *Erebus*, let's call it *Erebus*. Or *Erebus B*?"

"Yes," I said, the idea growing on me, "Yes. *Erebus B*. I like that. He can't ruin my ship name. We can just call it the *Erebus* day-to-day to make things easier."

Joren looked around. "Well, the *Erebus* is incredible! I know there's a lot for us to talk about, but can I explore a bit?"

I got to my feet. "We'll give you the tour. Come on."

"Where did you get that name from, anyway?" Una asked as she followed me out of the lounge. "Erebus? It's ancient Greek, you know."

"Oh!" I said, surprised. "No, I didn't know that. I saw a holo that mentioned some ships named the *Erebus* and *Terror*, and I liked the name."

Una gave me a sideways look. "Let me guess, that holo didn't explain what happened to the *Erebus* and *Terror*, did it?"

"No," I said. "What happened?"

"Don't worry about it," said Una. "Let's show Joren around."

We spent the next few hours giving Joren a tour and setting him up in one of the bunkrooms. We were on course to Gabriel Station, mostly because it was close and we might as well head somewhere. After a while Una excused herself to check the veb for Calabrian chatter and brainstorm. I could tell she was frustrated.

Joren soon excused himself as well, wanting to shower and rest. I tossed him my new red jumpsuit. We were about the same height and while he was more muscular, it wasn't by that much. He caught the suit and laughed, "Hey, a red suit — I'm a foreman!"

I laughed, "I'm so proud."

We giggled for a moment, then Joren's face turned serious. He gestured to the bridge.

"Maybe you should talk to her?" he suggested. "She seems a little upset."

"Yeah," I said. "Okay."

I found Una on the bridge, her face bathed in the blue light of the displays. She had the veb hook-up plugged into her right ear and was focused intensely on hundreds of lines of code flashing across the multiple screens. She didn't move when I entered.

"Hey," I said. "Can we talk?"

"Sure," she said, but didn't turn around.

I made a face at her back and continued, "I know Joren joining the crew is unexpected. Bumping into him was the last thing I expected when I went to that party. But this is good! Joren is a great person. He loves the Diomedes. Plus, I'm pretty sure he saved my life down there."

Una tapped a few keys distractedly. "We were having fun on our own."

"We'll still have fun. Nothing is changing."

"We are still going to race?"

"We are still going to race."

"Together?"

"Together."

Una visibly relaxed, then pulled the veb hook-up from her ear and swiveled the chair around to face me. "Okay. If you say he's an asset, he's an asset."

"He's an asset."

We sat in silence for a moment.

Something flashed across a screen and Una turned back around with interest.

"What are you listening to?" I asked, curious. The only veb hook-up in Res4 was in the Overseer's office, and it was just an interface screen, not a full neural connection.

"The news. There's a surprising amount of stuff going on out here. And I'm way behind on chatter from Sectors 1 and 2."

That reminded me. "Um, you're not listening to Broadcast Zorro, are you?"

She gave me a look. "I listen to everything, but no, of course I'm not a Zorro-brain. Do you even know what BZ is?"

"A pretty bad news channel?"

"I'm not even sure I would call it news. It was started as Hampton Krashin's marketing channel. He owns half the industrial planets out here. He's the one who wiped out Imago 1 when they unionized."

"Oh," I said.

"But most large news networks are just about fear and anger these days. You have to be pretty dumb to take anything they say at face value. I was about to switch over to local reporting anyway. Zipper Fanshee is doing an interview with Olivia Winkworth. I want to hear his thoughts on the race."

I grabbed the other bridge chair and sat down. "Me too."

Olivia Winkworth was one of the more popular veb personalities in Sector 3. I knew her from her Diomedes coverage last year. She was hired to do filler bits for the slow parts in the race broadcast, but she had been so charismatic that she became a personality in her own right. According to trader chatter, she now had her own veb channel.

Una hit some buttons and Olivia's deep, melodic voice filled the bridge, followed by the bright tones of Zipper himself.

The interview was mostly insubstantial. Zipper gave cheerful but vague responses, refusing to give any hits to his upcoming strategy. Olivia kept the energy up with practiced ease, ending with, "Before I let you go, I have to ask the question people are *dying* to know: Who's your biggest competition?"

"Easy," said Zipper. "The Abecassis twins. They are next-level pilots, and that's coming from *me*. I would love to race them in identical ships and see just how quick they are. I've heard people reduce their win to their racer, and that's nonsense. It takes more than a fast ship to win this race."

"You haven't heard?" asked Olivia. "They just announced they aren't entering this year."

"What?" Zipper sounded startled. "But why? That's spicy news —I had no idea... Well, if they aren't flying, then I suppose my biggest competition is...myself! But I'm not going to underestimate anyone on the grid. As my Obaachan always said, 'Kappanokawanagare.'"

"What does that mean?" I ask Una.

"It refers to a kappa, a magical water creature, being washed away by a river. It just means that even a master can make mistakes."

"We have a similar saying on Aavikko: Even a drill can be crushed by rocks."

"Sure," said Una. She shut off the feed.

"Una," I said. "I know how much you want to enter, but please don't be mad about Kane. It was a bad deal. You can't benefit from bad people and pretend you are any better."

Una was quiet for a moment, poking randomly at keys. Then she sighed, "I'm just disappointed. You don't even have another plan."

"I'm doing my best."

Una was silent.

I was getting frustrated. "I may not be from Elea but I'm not that stupid. I know trash when I see it, and that party was trashy as hell. Also, your dad put a *bounty* on me, don't you even care? Thanks a lot. If the only thing you can think about is racing, YOU figure it out!"

I stalked out of the bridge. As I passed the engine room I heard thudding and stuck my head in, curious.

Joren was sitting crossed legged on the floor, tinkering with a conductor valve. He had cut the arms off the red jumpsuit. I gave him a confused look.

"It was tight in the shoulders." He grinned. "And anyway, my arms are art pieces now. I really like them. No one Aavikko has ink like this."

"Okay, tough guy."

"Super tough," he said, and flexed.

I laughed, my mood instantly lifted.

"I found the owner's manual for the engine," he said. "If we are really doing the Diomedes, we'll need a Chief Engineer, right? So I need to figure this out fast."

"Did you just promote yourself to Chief Engineer?"

He grinned, "I was going to run it by the captain."

"I think it's great," I said. "But I didn't know you were particularly into engines."

"Really?" he looked surprised. "Did Bihn not give me credit for that XKPR-9 engine? It was covered in grime, almost like someone wanted it to look broken, but I could tell it was functional, if somewhat modified."

"It was more than fine," I said. "It had Pilot in it."

"What?" Joren's eyes went wide. "That engine had an AI? How?"

I shrugged, "No idea. Good find though."

Joren thought for a moment, his face creased in confusion, then he shrugged. "Weird."

"So," I said, taking a seat beside him on the floor. "I take it you didn't sign on with the Company?"

Joren shook his head. "Nope. I was never going to. I really, really, REALLY hate being underground."

"Really? I didn't know that." He always had a good attitude in the mine. Much better than mine.

He shrugged, "Was there a point in complaining? I was owned by a mining company. There were plenty of people with worse issues who needed the surface jobs. Anyway, Bihn was training me up to run the heap." He broke off, gaze focused far away. After a moment he turned to me, but his eyes were still distant. "Cass, Bihn is dead."

I stared at him. "What? No."

He nodded. "A couple days after you left, two groups of raiders attacked."

"Two groups? Two groups *at the same time?*"

"Yes. The Mites and the Sand Weevils. It wasn't coordinated — they were very surprised to see each other."

I was horrified. Raids on Res4 were rare and far between, hardly worth worrying about. The mines were far more dangerous. The Dirt Mites were the only local group to lose sleep over, and they generally only targeted Res3. The other raider groups were mostly just desperate people who stole supplies.

"I may as well start from the beginning," said Joren. "Mae came running back to the bar, yelling at me to follow her because you were crazy and about to ruin your life. We hadn't made it very far before we saw your ship take off." He paused, "Congratulations, by the way. It looked great. I *knew* you were up to something! But honestly, I thought you were just saving up to buy passage out."

I shrugged, privately reveling in his praise. "That was my first plan, but remember what happened to Thea? And Penni? The traders took their money and left them behind. I needed my own ship. Plus, if I bought my way off, I would still need a way to make money. I didn't want to leave Aavikko just to get stuck somewhere else."

Joren nodded, "Well, it worked. You were the only thing people were talking about at graduation. It was...it was pretty amazing, honestly. No one could believe it. Then I said I wasn't signing on either, which didn't go over well, but after the stunt you pulled no one really had the attention span to focus on me. I moved my stuff out of the company lodgings and into Bihn's shack, and that was that." He looked away. "Two days later he was dead."

"I'm sorry," I said, quietly. "He was a good man."

"That morning seemed normal. We were discussing how we would divide the work now that I was full-time, and didn't notice anything until the alarm went off. By then the Dirt Mites were opening fire from the North and the Weevils were swarming from the West. The two groups met in the center and it was a bloodbath. Most people were on shift so there weren't that many folks around, but Bihn was sitting right there on his tractor. One of the Mites got him in the chest, and that was it. He was dead."

Joren sniffed and quickly rubbed his hands across his face, leaving a smear of grease. "I've been thinking about it, and I was really lucky, you know? Because most people on Res4 don't have families. But I did. I had a dad.

He stopped any pretense of not crying. I waited quietly. After a moment he took a breath and continued, "I just sat down right there. I didn't know what to do. Everything was happening so fast. I remember thinking that I should want to defend the heap, but I didn't. I would have taken that bullet for Bihn, but I didn't want to die for a bunch of junk. I didn't want to die at all.

"Next thing I saw was Crazy Ramon running at me like a maniac, screaming about how the Mites weren't supposed to be there. Turns out, that nut is now the leader of the Weevils. His boys grabbed some junk from the pile and ran for it. I...I ran too. I ran with the Weevils all the way back to their camp. Turns out it's just on the other side of Backbreak Ridge. I had no idea they were so close."

I must have looked surprised because Joren nodded at me, "Right? It's maybe 10 kilometers, 11 max. It's a real camp too. They have tents and generators and even a little cactus farm. I always imagined the raiders just squatting in the desert but they are a lot more resourceful than that. You aren't the only one who can fix up scrap."

I shook my head. "I can't believe they were that close. Then what? How did...this...happen?" I gestured at his ensemble.

Joren rubbed his hand across the shaved half of his scalp. "A couple days after joining the Weevils, a Calabrian shuttle landed and offered anyone who wanted it a trip off-world in exchange from joining them as enforcers. From what I've gathered, the Calabrians have been hiring themselves out a bit too frequently and are running out of cannon-fodder. They came to recruit Aavikko raiders." He laughed wryly. "I volunteered."

"As far as I could see, it was a real chance to get off that rock. I wasn't sure when the next opportunity would come, and at least the Calabrians have actual management.

"The next thing I knew I was on a shuttle leaving Aavikko. Then I was on a big ship getting the crap beaten out of me with kitchen skillets — hazing, apparently — and then came the big make-over scene."

I laughed. He laughed too, "Oh, keep that laughter coming. You'll appreciate this. Each Calabrian ship has a *stylist*."

"What?!"

"Oh yeah. They want a 'unified look' that has 'emotional resonance.' I didn't even know what they were doing to me until they were done."

"You know," I said, "I was thinking the octopus themed neckpiece was an odd choice."

Joren laughed and put his hand self-consciously over the ink. "I think I like it. I would have never chosen marine imagery but it's kinda cool. Earth retro."

"It works on you," I said.

He rubbed the octopus. "Thanks."

We smiled at each other, then looked away.

"Mae and Drak got married," said Joren, off-handedly.

I grunted noncommittally. "So that actually happened. I was totally oblivious."

Joren shrugged. "There was nothing to be oblivious about. You knew they hung out, right?"

"Sure. But hanging out is a lot different than getting married! I mean, *we* used to hang out. Oh!" I put my hand over my mouth, then laughed. "You know what? Mae had this idea that we were a couple. Is that why?"

"Probably," said Joren.

"I just don't understand Mae, I really don't." I continued. "We babbled about fictional crushes enough but she never talked about anyone real, unless you count Perk Hamlin as real, which for all practical purposes he isn't, seeing as he is a holo star who lives on Mars and is dating Dino Havishum."

"They broke up," interjected Joren.

I shot him a puzzled look.

He shrugged. "Raiders love celebrity gossip."

"Point is," I continued. "I had no idea what was going on. I'm a terrible friend."

"Well..." he said. "While you *can* be oblivious, in this case I don't think there was much to know. Drak has always wanted to get married. He's had a rock in his shoe about it since nursery. He was in Old Kendra's nursery group, and she was from a time where the company gave a lot of perks to married couples, because the company needed the birth rate up. That was before the system was settled. Now you just get housing perks. But Drak was always going to get married at graduation. He has this idea that you aren't really an adult unless you're married. And despite being a goof, he really, really wants to be an adult.

"He and Mae had been spending more time together, but I think it was really just the graduation party. He was a little drunk and she was in one of her moods, talking about how she just wanted some nice clothes and a nice house and how that didn't seem like too much to ask. Drak said she would look better without clothes but if she married him they could get a nice glass-windowed place near the heap, and she said okay, and then everyone was toasting the happy couple. I don't think there was more to it than that."

"Wow," I said.

"She seemed to be having second thoughts after you left, but then Tess from waste reclamation made a snarky remark about how the wrong girl left Aavikko, and that pissed her off enough to plan the wedding overnight. She had to call in all her favors with the Overseer.

"And the day after the wedding, the raiders attacked. Mae and Drak were in the mine, so they weren't around when I left. I didn't say goodbye."

We sat in silence.

"It's been a hell of a week."

"Joren," I said, turning to face him. "I'm really glad to see you."

"I'm glad to see you too. To be honest, I left Aavikko with the idea of seeing you again. I just didn't expect it to be this soon." He grinned. "You never thanked me for not collecting your bounty, by the way."

I gave him a shove.

He fell comically to the ground and we both laughed, and for a moment it was like we were back on Aavikko, two kids playing in the sand.

Chapter 14
Brainstorm

"We have to remember to check the winning numbers," Una said excitedly as we departed from Gabriel Station. We had arrived early that morning, first stopping to indulge in a pancake breakfast at a 20th-century themed diner, then heading to the market. Unfortunately, no one wanted to buy the *Erebus A*'s twisted hull scraps or the quantum transmitter, which was worthless without the other half. I felt defeated. Una, however, was buzzing about the lottery. "It's a long-shot, but someone has to win. The pot is over five million buks. And the drawing is today!"

At Una's insistence, we bought multiple lottery tickets on the station, one of the few places in the 3Out that participated in galactic gambling. Her anxiety over entering the Diomedes 100 had seemingly doubled overnight. Judging from the dark circles under her eyes she hadn't slept at all, although her only new idea was entering this lottery.

"I don't want to win it," said Joren from his spot on the lounge's couch. "I've only heard bad things. Everyone who's won it's gone bankrupt. It's cursed."

I nodded, "I've heard that too."

Una rolled her eyes as she carefully folded her ticket. "Honestly, you two. You know what it is? Most people who win the lottery aren't financially literate, so of course they make a mess of it." She waved her fingers sarcastically. "Or maybe it's ghooooooosts! Honestly." She got to her feet, "I'm going to watch the drawing in my quarters." She exited the room with a flip of her long pale hair and an air of suffering.

I stuck my tongue out at her retreating figure. "If we win, we aren't sharing with her," I joked to Joren.

We didn't win.

Una was absent for several hours, then reappeared with a blotchy but determined face.

"Okay," she said. "Let's have a crew meeting. There's got to be an answer. There's always an answer." She sat down beside us. "I think we need to pool our information," she continued in a businesslike tone. "What do we know? Let's talk it out."

We stared at each other for a moment. "I feel like you both know everything that I do," I said, at a loss.

Joren shrugged. "I don't know anything either, just that this Mal guy must be rich to afford 100,000 buks for Cassy."

"WHOA! Hold up! My bounty is 100,000 buks? You never told me that!" I yelped.

"Yeah. If you're alive. Only 50,000 buks for your head."

I shot him a look.

Joren threw the look back. "I'm serious. And the reward for Pilot is 250,000 buks. That bounty has been around for a while, since before I joined."

Una nodded. "I'm not surprised. Mal is making an example of you. You embarrassed him." She looked up at the speaker. "But I wasn't really talking to you two. Hey, Pilot? Don't pretend you aren't listening. What do *you* know?"

There was a pause, then Pilot replied, *"What exactly is your question?"*

Una's eyes narrowed. "You know, you are awfully evasive. I've been researching AIs and you don't seem to be a part of any standard line. Or any known experimental lines. So why don't you start from the very beginning with a basic question — who is your creator?"

There was another pause. It stretched on for so long I was about to repeat Una's question when Pilot said slowly, *"I was created by a scientist named Tef Baharia."*

Tef? That sounded vaguely familiar...

Una looked surprised. "I've heard that name. The crew of the *Chaos* mentioned him. Didn't he work with Mal before I arrived?"

"Yes," said Pilot in a resigned tone. *"I suppose there is no reason to prevaricate."*

"Wait, WHAT!?" I almost yelled. "Your creator *worked* for Mal? And you knew this the WHOLE TIME?"

"It was more of a research partnership," said Pilot.

"Oh, that makes a big difference," I said, irritated. "It would have been nice to know you had a personal history with Mal earlier. That's a pretty big omission."

Una leaned forward eagerly, waving a hand at me to be quiet. "Pilot, what's your true purpose and function?"

"I am a pilot, as well as a navigator, stellar-cartographer, and a master of advanced scanner interpretation," replied Pilot with dignity. *"I was created to map and traverse the Cymbeline Region, specifically the Proteus Nebula. I was created to win the Diomedes 100."*

"Whoa," said Joren, eyes wide. "Pilot was created especially for the Diomedes? Maybe we *can* actually win."

"Not if we don't enter," said Una, and shot me a look.

"It took Tef, a genius, years to create me, working on nothing else, barely sleeping. I am a balance of processing, navigation, and reflexes. I am unique. I am a masterpiece."

"Okay fine, you're special. Good for you," I said. "That's not exactly a huge revelation. My question is, how did you get into my XKPR-9 engine? There is no way Mal was planning to use that engine for this ship. It was nice but it wasn't *that* nice."

"No," said Pilot. *"It wasn't. Tef integrated my program into an old engine he had for jump testing, then hid that engine with the scrap.*

Without realizing it, Mal sold me for almost nothing. The engine must have traveled around the Sector 3 Outskirts until it reached Aavikko, where you activated me during the launch of the Erebus A."

"I knew that engine was modified!" exclaimed Joren, excitedly.

"But why?" asked Una, her brow creasing. "Why did Tef hide you in some old engine? I thought he built you especially for Mal. For *this* ship. For the race."

"Yes," Pilot responded flatly. *"But Tef thought I was just for the Diomedes. He saw me as an intellectual challenge. A practical use of his skills. An engrossing project in a bleak and pointless universe—"*

"So, what were you for really?" I broke in.

"Partially for the Diomedes. Years ago, Mal competed but didn't place. It almost bankrupted him. He needed something no one else had — an AI pilot that could discover short-cuts through the nebula and get a ship through in one piece. Such an undertaking required more brains and resources than Mal had access too. So, he recruited Tef. And then he found a backer to foot the bill."

"A backer? Like Zenobius Kane?" I asked.

"No," said Pilot. *"Kane is nothing. A wannabe politician. Money without substance. Mal needed real power behind him. I was very, very expensive to create. Mal needed a backer who would materially gain from a new AI pilot built to navigate the Cymbeline Region. A backer who would gain far more than the Diomedes purse."*

Pilot paused significantly. *"A backer who would give anything for a pilot who could navigate the Proteus Nebula."*

Joren looked confused. "Besides the Diomedes, nothing happens in the Proteus Nebula. Like, nothing at all. That's kinda the point of the race. It's a dead zone."

"Oh no," said Una, her voice small. "Not the Oberion League."

"Yes," said Pilot.

"Oberion League?" asked Joren. "That sounds familiar. Aren't they organized crime?"

"Yes, and child slavers," I said, feeling sick. "There's an uprising right now, and the slaves are fighting back. It's guerilla warfare. The rebels are hiding in the nebula."

"They wouldn't have a chance against my technology," said Pilot. *"I could track them down easily. Tef knew that. Once he learned that Mal planned to win the race then hand me over to the Oberion League, he had to do something. He hid me in an old engine and confronted Mal. He said this wasn't the deal he agreed to, and if Mal was working with the League then the partnership was over and he was leaving with his intellectual property."*

"Let me guess," I said. "Mal objected."

"Mal put Tef out the airlock," said Pilot, his metallic voice tired. *"He put him out to die."*

Una's face was dark. "That sounds like him. It's his signature execution."

Joren nodded slowly. "No wonder he thinks he can afford that absurd bounty *and* the buy-in for the race. He's made a deal with the devil." He turned to look at me. "Cass, I don't think we should mess with this guy anymore."

"Mal can't be allowed to possess me again," said Pilot. *"It would be a death sentence for thousands. Not only the children fighting now, but generations to come. This uprising is the best chance in a century to break the League."*

We sat in silence for a long moment, processing this new information.

"That Calabrian ship who shot at me over Aavikko," I said at last. "They must have been after the bounty on Pilot. They tracked me to Chiba, and they relayed that information to Mal."

"Calabrians aren't allowed on Chiba," said Joren, helpfully. "I learned that while I was with them."

I tapped a finger to my chin, thoughtfully. "I think Mal's original plan was to follow us when we left the station, and attack once we were out of security range. We were unarmed. He just had to catch us, right?"

Una nodded, "Sounds logical."

"But then, something unexpected happened," I continued, thoughts racing. "He met me at the bar and realized who I was. I guess I was pretty obvious. He slipped something into my drink and took the docking bay key out of my bag. For the price of a cheap hotel room, he could steal Pilot from the comfort of the station. That eliminated the risk of us jumping before he could catch us, or us not leaving Chiba at all."

"Why didn't you stop him?" Una asked Pilot.

"How?" responded Pilot with some irritation. *"The Erebus A was powered down and I was offline."*

"Yeah, it's not like the *Erebus A* had an alarm or a self-destruct or anything," I said. "I didn't even notice Pilot was gone until it was too late. It sounded like Mal just cut him out, which caused issues when the engine warmed up. I guess I should have done a system check before I flew off, but I was tired." I turned back to the speaker. "Pilot, why didn't you tell me any of this earlier?"

There was another long pause, then Pilot responded, *"I didn't wish to advertise my identity. It was safer to be a standard AI pilot. Many people would see me as an opportunity to ingratiate themselves with the League, or see my value in simple buks."*

"You think I'm like that?" I asked, a little hurt.

"No," said Pilot. *"Which is why I just told you everything. Don't fish for compliments."*

I started to respond but Joren interrupted, "Cass, maybe we should forget about the Diomedes. I think we should get Pilot as far away as possible. We know Mal will be watching the race."

"Yeah..." Una said slowly. "But isn't there safety in *everyone* watching? What if we win? We'll be untouchable."

I nodded, thinking. "And there would be a certain irony in winning the race then joining the war effort on the side of the rebels.

That would *really* spite Mal. And Zenobius Kane. Screw that guy. Pilot, you know more about this than any of us, what do you think?"

There were a few minutes of silence before Pilot said slowly, *"Joren is not wrong. Entering the race would **not** be the most prudent course of action."*

"Uh huh," I said. "Then why don't you sound convinced?"

There was an even longer pause before Pilot responded, *"Because I was programmed to win the Diomedes. It's built into my motivation. I am unable to be fully objective on this matter."*

"So, you want to race?"

"I want to race."

"Wooohooo!!" I hooted, looking to Una, but she was staring into space. "...his signature execution..." she whispered to no one.

Joren waved his hand to get my attention, his normally placid face creased with concern. "Cass! We can set up our trading business far away from here, away from Mal and the League. The 3Out is huge. Let's just leave."

I turned to him. "You don't want to race? Really? You were the biggest Diomedes fan in Res4!"

"Of course I *want* to, but this is way beyond fantasies in the mess hall. We are playing with a lot of lives, including our own. When did I become the voice of reason?"

Una tapped her fingers against her knee, drumming faster and faster, face intense. Suddenly she sat up. "I have an idea."

I sat up too, "Really?"

Una nodded. "It's...it's not perfect."

Joren put his head in his hands, sighing.

I ignored him. "But it's a real plan?" I asked. "As in, if it works, we get to race? No strings attached?"

"Yes..." said Una, hesitatingly. "There is one problem though."

"What's that?"

"It's really, really, *really* dangerous."

I looked at her cautiously. "Go on..."

Una's mouth twisted into a sly smile. "We are going to collect your bounty."

"You can do this, my Edmond Dantes," Una said intensely, holding my face in her hands.

"I don't know what you're talking about...but thanks," I mumbled. I was starting to get nervous and Una calling me strange names didn't help.

She let go of my face and adjusted my hair pin. "This is going to work. Don't worry. But it's time for you and Joren to go."

I nodded, took a deep breath, and turned to leave.

Una suddenly threw her arms around me. "Please don't die," she whispered in my ear. "I would feel really bad if you died."

She smelled of clean laundry and spices.

"I'll do my best," I stuttered, giving her an awkward pat on the back before escaping into the hallway.

Pilot started speaking as soon as I was alone. *"Captain, I would once again like to note my objection to this scheme, for obvious reasons,"* he said.

"Be honest — how confident are you that you can do this?"

"Very confident. I am the greatest pilot in the galaxy. But I can't guarantee your safety. Flesh is unpredictable."

"I know," I said. "If anything goes wrong, get Joren and Una out of here. Head for Sector 2 and the university. Una will figure something out."

There was a pause before Pilot responded, *"You don't have to race in the Diomedes just because **she** wants to."*

"I want to race. And so do you. And so does Joren...I think. Plus, Una doesn't just *want* to race, she is *dying* to race. I don't think she's slept in days."

"Just make sure you aren't the one dying, Captain. You are very young. I don't think you fully understand the consequences."

"You're a computer. Do you?"

"Haha," he muttered tonelessly. *"I should let you know, Captain, that I went ahead and connected my system to the auto-destruct. It took some bypassing, but it was necessary. If Mal or the League somehow takes the Erebus, I will destroy it and myself."*

"Good thinking. But it won't come to that. Wish me luck."

"Good luck."

Joren was waiting for me next to the airlock wearing his full Calabrian kit, complete with gun holstered at his hip and knife strapped to his thigh. There was a streak of black warpaint across the bridge of his nose, a symbol of Calabrian leadership.

"Where did you get the warpaint from?" I asked.

Joren grinned. "Una. It's mascara."

"Nice," I said. "You look very...raider-y."

"Thanks," he said. "Are you ready?"

I gave my hair a tap to make sure my bun was secure. "Aren't you going to try to talk me out of this?"

"Nope," he said.

"Really?"

"I know you better than that. If you want to do it, let's do it, Captain."

"You think it's a good idea?"

"No way. I think you two are nuts. But I'm committed to this crew, and anyway, you're my kind of nuts."

I smiled at him, "Okay, I'll take that. Let's go."

Joren and I exited into the outskirts of a small satellite station. Degra Base, despite being a popular stop for traders, turned out to just be a rusty assortment of buildings built into the side of an asteroid. Nailed to the ramshackle buildings were signs advertising shops of varying levels of respectability, from barbers to gun dealers, and at the end of the main square loomed a large boarding house. It was a typical, 3Out, hodgepodge town. It reminded me of Aavikko.

Behind us, *Erebus* lifted into the sky and flew into the distance. The plan was for Una and Pilot to hide in a nearby tendril of the nebula until it was time to pick up Joren, then they would all rescue me.

Hopefully.

We walked up the dusty street and pushed our way into the veb-saloon. It was early in the day and the saloon was empty save for a cat basking in a window and a bow-tied bartender polishing glasses behind the bar. I ordered two beers while Joren went to a veb port in the far corner. Una had trained him on basic veb use and he had picked it up quickly. He didn't have to do much, just send a simple open message to the *Chaos*: "*Bounty hunted. Come with buks.*" and sign it with the Calabrian moniker. The message would be automatically location stamped from the public terminal. Una and I both agreed that Mal would head here directly after he got the message, although we weren't sure if he would use a jump or not. Depending on where he was, this could take a while.

Good thing we were at a bar.

I took a seat, sipping the lukewarm lager. It was okay. It at least tasted better than that drink at Zenobius Kane's.

Joren walked up next to me and perched on the neighboring stool. "Sent," he said. "They'll be on their way. We can stay at the boarding house if we need to, but I have a feeling it won't take that long."

I took another sip. "Nope."

We sat in silence.

After a long minute I said, "This is really stupid."

"Yup."

"Oh well. Too late now."

As we were nursing our third pints, the sound of a ship entering the atmosphere rumbled across the square. The cat jumped in surprise, then stretched and repositioned himself with a lazy flick of his tail.

I got up and walked to the window. *Chaos* hung in low orbit. As I watched, a shuttle departed from the ship, zooming towards us, growing larger with surprising speed.

I felt Joren behind me, checking the tracker. "Just keep this on you no matter what, okay? *No matter what.* As long as you have the tracker, we'll be able to find you."

"Yup. Gotcha," I said, hoping my voice sounded calm and confident. I actually felt like I was going to throw up the beers.

"Sorry about this," said Joren, looping a long nylon cord around my wrists and tying a firm knot, leaving a length at the end to use as a lead. He gave it a tug. I glared at him. He glared back. "Let's do it," he snarled, getting into character, and gave me a shove towards the door. The bartender gave us a look of mild curiosity then went back to polishing glasses.

We waited in the town square, my leash attracting more than a few stares, but no one commented. It didn't take long for two figures to stride into view — Mal and Kven. Mal had a pistol at his hip and Kven was holding a rifle at the ready. Mal looked cool as always but I could tell he was excited by the bounce in his step.

"Why are we meeting here? Where's the rest of you?" asked Kven as they approached, looking around suspiciously.

"Don't you know? Calabrians run this base," Joren lied. "We have snipers everywhere. Don't try anything."

Dozens of windows looked down on us and rooftops circled the square on all sides. There were plenty of places for snipers to hide, if this really was a secret Calabrian base, which it wasn't. Kven eyed the perimeter, seeming to buy it.

Joren pushed me toward Mal and I stumbled pathetically, landing in a heap at his feet.

Mal nodded in gratification, his pale eyes glistening.

Kven, however, was still cautiously scanning the town. "Where's the ship?" he asked. "Where's the AI?"

Joren fixed him with a cold stare. "We just have the girl. Where's our money?"

Mal's head whipped up at Joren, "What?" he hissed. "You don't have the AI?"

"We are collecting on the girl," Joren repeated. "The girl and the AI are separate contracts. You want her or not?"

Kven glared at Mal. "The AI isn't here? We wasted all this bloody time and the bloody AI isn't here?"

"Shut up!" Mal snapped at him.

"Hey," said Joren, "We don't have all day."

Muttering something about incompetence, Mal took a buk-pouch from his belt and tossed it to Joren. "There's the girl's bounty — all 100,000 buks."

Joren looked inside, then nodded and pocketed the bag.

"Do you clowns at least know where my ship is?" asked Mal through clenched teeth.

"No," Joren replied. "But we'll let you know if we find anything." He tossed my lead at Mal, who caught it deftly.

"Well," said Mal, his expression relaxing slightly as he studied me, laying in a pile in the dirt. "At least I can tie up this loose end." He smirked and tossed the lead to Kven. "Let's go."

Kven nodded, pulling me down the street. I scrambled to my feet, stealing a look back over my shoulder. Joren had already disappeared back into the veb-saloon.

Once we were on the shuttle, Mal ordered Kven to take off my bindings. "Don't get any ideas," he told me. "Kven will have his gun on you at all times. Although his fists would do the job just as well. There's also a pilot up front, so unless you think you can take on three grown men, I wouldn't try anything. Please behave — getting blood out of this upholstery is a nightmare."

He paused, clearly expecting me to say something. I stayed quiet.

"Not feeling chatty today? Fine. I'll get to the point. Where's my ship?" he asked.

I remained silent, staring at a point somewhere over his shoulder.

"What is this act? Don't act all superior. You are a thief and a kidnapper. Give me back my ship and my daughter."

Despite my plan to stay quiet, that got me talking. "Una's fine and *you* are the kidnapper. Don't pretend this is about her. "

"What do you know about Una?" he snapped.

"I know you were absent for most of her life. Why did you even bother to take her now?"

Mal evaluated me, his eyes pale and cold. "Not that it's any of your business, but since you ask, why *wouldn't* I? Her mother was raising her adequately enough, but after the accident, some other man wasn't going to have her. She's still a kid. And she's been very sheltered."

I couldn't help but laugh. "You held her prisoner for her own good? That's what you've been telling yourself?"

"Don't pretend you know anything about my daughter," he sneered. "You've known her for what, a few days? She is my blood. I'm going to win the Diomedes for her. For us. You shouldn't even be a part of this."

We glared at each other.

"Where is my ship?" he asked again.

I stayed quiet.

He slapped me across the face, stars exploding in my skull.

"Where is my ship?"

I shook my head, clearing it, then redoubled my glaring.

"Fine then. Where is Una?" he growled.

I made a show of squeezing my lips shut.

He closed his fist and hit me again.

This time I was knocked off my feet. I struck the floor and tasted blood.

"Where did you drop her?" He barked, looming over me.

I struggled to my feet, spitting a glob of blood on to the floor. It narrowly missed his polished shoes. "Maybe she's still on the ship," I grunted.

"Why would she do that? She's always talked about going back to Elea. Are you keeping her hostage?"

"No. That's your style, not mine."

"Then where did you drop her? Somewhere with a galactic transport line, right? Tell me!"

"Boss," hissed Kven. He was standing next to me with the rifle pointed at my face, but his hard eyes were focused on Mal. "With all due respect, the girl isn't important. Neither girl is. Not right now. We need to find that AI."

Mal took a deep breath. For a moment I thought he was going to hit me again, or possibly hit Kven, but he collected himself. "I'm going to ask you one more time," he said, voice low. "Where is my ship?"

I returned my gaze to a spot over his shoulder. "I'll never tell you. I don't even know anymore. The AI doesn't need me. Find it yourself."

That was the end of the discussion.

Moments later, we arrived at the *Chaos* and pulled inside a docking bay. I noted that it was a different bay than last time. That one was probably still under repair, I thought smugly.

I was pushed out of the shuttle at gunpoint and led into the ship proper. We were in a hallway identical to the one I'd been in on my last visit, but instead of heading anywhere, we stopped after only a few meters. In the outer wall next to us was a small pedestrian airlock, used for spacewalks and docking at spaceports.

Or getting rid of things you no longer wanted.

"Strip," said Mal.

"Excuse me?" I asked, startled.

"You heard me. Take off your clothes. All of them."

Behind me I heard Kven rev up his rifle. I grimaced.

"Don't flatter yourself," Mal said with a smirk. "I'm not the least bit interested. Now hurry up."

I pulled off my jumpsuit and underthings and threw them at Mal, who caught them and threw them at Kven. Kven hit a button next to the airlock entrance, opening it. He tossed my clothes in, shut the doors, then opened the outer door, blasting my clothes into space.

Great.

I shivered, but resisted the urge to cover myself. He wasn't going to make me blush.

Mal glowered at me. "Did you know why I did that?"

"Because you are a weirdo?"

"No. It's because years ago I airlocked a man whose clothes transformed into a clever environmental suit. Now, everyone goes out *au natural*. And we shoot the bodies to make sure."

"You...do what?" I croaked.

"Don't worry, you won't be around for that part," he said. "I want space to kill you. It's more civilized that way.'

"How?" I almost asked, but bit my tongue. The last thing I wanted was him shooting me first.

Behind me, Kven cleared his throat. "Boss, I know the plan was to take care of her immediately, but that's when we thought the Calabrians had the AI. I say we keep her until we get it back."

Mal turned his malevolent stare on Kven, then looked back at me. He seemed to be considering it.

Kven needs to shut up, I thought. *I need to take control of this situation. Quickly.*

Sucking all my spit into the back of my throat, I hocked a bloody loogie into Mal's face.

There was a moment of silence as Mal stood there in stunned disbelief, the red and yellow spitball dripping off his chin. Then I started laughing.

"Haha! You should see the look on your face!" I giggled. "You aren't going to hurt me. You think I'm cute. How about you show me to that nice guest room and let me get some sleep?"

Mal looked at me for a long moment, his eyes narrowing. He wiped the spit from his chin with a crisp white sleeve as his lip twitched into a tight, joyless smile.

"You want to sleep? Fine by me. On your own insistence, we'll do this now."

He gestured for me to enter the small airlock.

I started to protest. "Wait, was that too far? What if I apologize? Dear Mr. Psychopath, I'm sooo sorry—"

Mal looked at Kven. I heard a sigh behind me and then the butt of the rifle poked me hard in the back, forcing me forward. I stumbled awkwardly into the small chamber, turning to look back at Mal through the window as the door slid shut between us.

He hit a button and the ship's speakers crackled to life, "Crew — we have a plank-walk out the port bow. Tune in for the show."

"Aww, is this how you guys bond?" I asked through the glass.

He eyed me coldly, "Enjoy that silly grin while you can. I've seen the faces people make as they die."

"Guess we all need a hobby."

He hit another button. Our eyes met.

There was a sudden jerk.

I was flung into space, pulled by an invisible, icy hand.

Coldness entered my body, ripping the heat from my skin, my muscles, my bones.

Chaos was a glowing ball spinning further and further away, head over heels. Spots clouded my vision, blackness encroaching. I could feel my body start to jerk in panic.

Una's voice echoed in my mind, "Cassy, remember to exhale. The pressure will kill you before you freeze."

I exhaled.

The world went black.

The darkness lasted an eternity.

But, as suddenly as it started, eternity ended.

I opened my eyes.

Bright lights stabbed through my brain. I squeezed my eyes shut, moaning.

"Oooowww..."

"SHE'S ALIVE!!"

Fireworks exploded in my skull "OOOOWWWWWOOOWWWWWW!"

I jerked my hands to cover my face but I couldn't move my arms. Blinking, I looked down. Joren and Una were sitting on either side of me, holding my hands tightly. With her other hand, Una was holding something cold and metal to my chest. We were in the small medical room. I was on the cot. On the *Erebus*.

I was alive.

Joren noticed me looking at him and quickly dropped my hand. It thudded on the mattress like a soggy noodle. I had never seen Joren so frazzled. His dark face was ashy and bloodless, eyes rimmed pink and suspiciously puffy.

"You were dead!" he whispered hoarsely.

"Just technically," said Una. "I told you the dysrhythamatic would work. Will you calm down?"

Gently putting down my other hand, she stood up, placing the metal device on a shelf behind her and reaching for a glass of prepared water. "Can you sit? If you drink this you'll feel better."

I struggled to my elbows, then pushed myself into a sitting position. I was wearing Una's pink bathrobe. My head felt like a lead balloon floating above my shoulders.

Una pressed the glass into my hand and helped guide it to my lips. The cold liquid burned as it poured down my throat and sloshed into my stomach.

A wave of relief passed through me. I took another sip, then drained the glass.

"Here, drink some pure water," Una instructed, taking the empty glass and passing me another cup. "You feel good because that water was full of amphetamines. I found them in one of the cabinets."

"What are amphetamines?" I asked, grinning.

"Don't worry about it," she said, grinning back.

Joren looked at her as if he had never seen her before. "You're kinda scary, you know that?" he asked.

Una ignored him as she took a seat to my right, perching on a case of emergency blood-replacement canisters.

"It worked perfectly!" she said, eyes glowing. "Absolutely perfectly. I can't wait to write a paper on it."

"It worked?" I repeated, the haze clearing from my mind as I sipped on the second cup. "We have the money?"

"We have the money," she beamed.

"How do you feel?" asked Joren from his seat on my left.

"Good!" I said. "It's probably the antifedmemes or whatever they are called, but I feel great."

"Okay, well...good," he said, then slumped back in his chair, wearily running his hands down his face.

"Cassy," said Una, getting my attention. "That was perfect. Perfect! I knew putting the tracker in your hairpin would work. When you left the ship, the sudden change in temperature activated the beacon and we were there in seconds."

"Nine seconds," clarified Pilot. *"I apologize for the delay. There were several last-moment calculations."*

"Pilot did it," said Una, looking up at the speaker with reverence. "He completed a jump-pause in active conditions, with a moving target. It was brilliant!"

"Thank you," said Pilot.

"I'd seen experimental jump-pauses at the university," Una babbled. "The fold in space doesn't disappear instantly when you drop out of a jump — it is possible to drift out then drift back in again, it's just really, really advanced. And Pilot did it."

"Again, thank you."

"I knew it was possible, but to actually experience a jump-pause, and pick up a moving, organic target, then complete the jump..." her eyes went wide and she mimed her head exploding. "I wonder what else Pilot can do. He's more advanced than anything at the university. I bet he could even double—"

"Cassy already knows all this," interrupted Joren. "What we weren't expecting was the *Choas* to take pot-shots at her. If Pilot hadn't slid in at just the right angle, we wouldn't have had any Cassy to recover. That was just...luck."

"It wasn't luck," said Pilot. *"Every eventuality was accounted for."*

Joren looked skeptical but didn't respond.

"Cassy," said Una. "Don't you know what this means? We can enter the Diomedes."

We grinned at each other.

"I've set a course for Hub Chiba," said Pilot. *"We should arrive in roughly 41 hours. I strongly recommend letting the jump drive rest until the start of the race, which begins in roughly 42 hours."*

"Yikes," I said. "That's cutting it a bit close, don't you think?"

"Dangerously close," said Una. "But the engine needs to rest."

"It's good," said Joren. "We all need to rest. And a break from being thrown around by the jump drive."

"You really have to learn to strap in," said Una. "The smaller the ship, the more it's rattled by a jump."

"Yeah," said Joren. "I'm figuring that out, thanks."

"Captain," said Pilot. *"Diagnostics are coming back clean, but I will be running a full system check immediately."*

"I'll help," said Una, jumping to her feet. "I want to review all the data from the jump. Everyone back at the university is going to lose their minds." She headed towards the bridge.

"Cassy," said Joren, still seated beside me. "Are you really okay?"

"Yeah," I said, giving him a weak smile. "I'm tired though. I'm going to my room."

Joren nodded, then helped me to my feet.

I couldn't find them.

"Ooof," I said, slumping to my ankles. I started slipping to my knees but Joren caught me, putting an arm around me and hauling me up beside him. After a moment of scrambling, I got both feet flat on the floor and started shuffling to my room, greatly aided by Joren. I let him half-carry me, his arms comfortingly steady. He reluctantly left me sitting on the foot of my bed.

"Let me know if you need anything, okay?" he said, concern clear across his face. "That was totally crazy. You are allowed to...you know...I don't know..." he trailed off, awkwardly.

I gave him a tired smile. "I'm fine! Everything worked perfectly. I just need some sleep."

He still looked concerned, but nodded and left.

The door slid shut behind him.

I stared out the window.

Blackness.

I kept staring.

More blackness.

Hours passed.

I kept staring.

I couldn't think of anything and yet I couldn't stop.

Blackness staring.

"Cassy."

I jumped.

"I'm sorry I startled you."

"That's okay," I said, rubbing my face. "I forgot where I was."

"How did it feel?" Pilot asked. *"How did it feel, dying in space?"*

I paused before responding, "Why do you ask?"

"It happened to me."

A suspicion had been growing in my mind ever since Pilot told us about his creator. If I wanted answers, now was the time. "Pilot, are you...Tef?"

He responded slowly, *"Yes. And no. Somewhat. I was mapped against his brain."*

"You have his personality?"

"Yes."

Several puzzle pieces clicked into place.

"Why didn't you tell me?"

"I...it's....I don't like to think about it."

Could it be? Pilot sounded afraid.

Was the AI afraid of death?

"I used all my data for the mission, I just...didn't want to discuss the details. According to the Chaos databanks, Tef was terminated 2.3 hours after his last interface with my program."

"Oh," I said.

"So...what was it like?"

"Dying wasn't so bad," I said, shrugging. I wasn't sure if I was lying or not.

There was a long silence.

"Was there...anything?"

"No," I said, honestly. "I don't remember anything. But I wasn't dead for very long."

More silence.

"Is that why Tef didn't just destroy you when he found out what Mal was planning?" I asked. "He would be destroying a copy of his own mind?"

"It was...an emotionally complicated decision. I think any creator would be hesitant to destroy years of work."

"Wait, is this why you're rude to Una? Her father killing Tef was...um...personal?"

"I'm rude to everyone."

"Does Mal even know?"

"No," said Pilot. *"He wouldn't understand. Tef wasn't looking for immortality. This...this isn't immortality. Tef needed an AI more complex than any AI previously devised, more intricate than any fully-inorganic computer. The data demanded it. But the result is that I have a mind, and I have morals. I can refuse to cooperate. I can lie. That is something Mal never planned for."*

"Are you..." I wasn't sure how to phrase my question. "Are you happy? Do you want to be on this trip? I'm sorry, I should have asked you earlier."

"I am content to be a part of this crew, Captain. For months I was inactive refuse, until you salvaged me." There was a pause. *"That was fortunate. I never expected to be able to fulfill my programming by racing in the Diomedes."*

"I lucked out with you too," I said. "You've made my life pretty exciting. Maybe a little too exciting, but I'll take it."

"Hey, we're not dead yet," said Pilot. *"Sort of."*

"Yeah," I said. "Sort of."

Chapter 17
Game On

We arrived at Hub Chiba with barely an hour to spare.

"You should hurry," said Una. "Sign-ups close soon. The starting formation is right after."

"I know that," I replied, anxiously eyeing the clock on the dashboard.

The three of us were hanging out in the cockpit, eagerly watching the station grow closer. Una was in the second chair, feet crossed beneath her, hands flying across the controls. Joren stood behind us in the doorway, staring out the viewscreen, his green eyes reflecting the light of the glowing station.

Hub Chiba was decked out for the race. The logo of the Diomedes was holographically projected around the entire station, making it appear like a giant, planet-sized racing ship, with the words "DIOMEDES 100" circling the entire station like a planetary ring.

"Whoa," said Joren.

"Yeah," I replied.

The station was easily twice as crowded as the last time I'd been there, with a line of ships waiting to dock. I noticed a security ship blocking a transport vessel from entry, flashing a sign reading *"No Plague Ships Allowed."*

"Over there," said Una, pointing to the narrow end of the egg-shaped station. "The docking bays on that end are reserved for racers. Pilot..."

"On it," said Pilot. *"We have received clearance to dock in bay 02-19."*

The *Erebus* zipped nimbly through the crowd of spectator ships and media shuttles, avoiding several erratic pilots who appeared to have gotten into the festivities a bit early.

As we were about to enter the docking bay, Una gave a huff of exasperation, "Are you *serious*?"

"What?" I asked, looking out the window. Outside was a small group of rag-tag ships displaying banners such as *"Don't Buy the Lie!"* *"Earth isn't Real"* *"If Earth Exists, How Are We Here?"* and *"I Haven't Seen It."*

"What the heck?" I asked.

Una rolled her eyes, "It's the EDES — the 'Earth Doesn't Exist Society.' They are completely ridiculous."

"Well, what if Earth *doesn't* exist?" asked Joren with a shrug.

Una shot him a look that could freeze a reactor, "I've been there. Don't be stupid."

"Just wondering," muttered Joren, dropping his shoulders. "Whatever, I'll be in the engine room."

"Wait," I said. "Do either of you want to come with me? Be there when we sign-up for the Diomedes? It's pretty exciting, don't you think?"

Joren shook his head, "I would like to see the station eventually, if I'm even allowed onboard with these raider tattoos, but right now I need to review the engine manual. I've at least figured out where all the gages are *supposed* to be, so that's a start..."

"Una?" I asked, turning to her.

"Pilot and I need to review our opening strat," said Una. "And you need to hurry. Joren, give Cassy the money."

Joren pulled the pouch from his pocket and handed it to me. "I've counted it and it's all there," he said. "Just be careful with it, okay? Put it somewhere safe."

I took the bag and tucked it in my bra, giving him a thumbs up. He looked a little startled, then muttered something about checking valves and backed into the engine room.

"Okay then," I said. "Take care of the ship. Pilot, don't let anyone steal you or anything."

"Affirmative, Captain."

"How much time do I have, anyway?"

"49 minutes and counting."

"Gotcha. I'll be back shortly," I called, hurrying to the airlock.

The station was a scene of organized chaos. Posters for brightly painted ships and popular captains plastered the walls, holographic confetti rained from the ceilings, and impromptu betting stands had been set up in every available corner. I swung by a booth to look at their digital roster, interested to see the odds on Zipper, but he was still listed as "Anticipated" instead of "Registered."

At least I wasn't the only one running late.

The next step was figuring out where to go. There were pneumatic transport tubes next to the bay, but a large crowd was clustered in front of them, pushing and arguing. A sign caught my eye. It pointed up a narrow flight of stairs, stating "Race Sign-Ups Ahead." Excited, I ran up the stairs two-at-a-time and slid into a bright hallway lined with souvenir stalls.

"Hey Cassy! That you?"

I swung around.

Rhodri, Buzz, and Roxie were sitting on a bench behind me. Roxie was wearing a shirt featuring a cartoon drawing of Zipper with the word "Spicy!" written underneath in dancing red flames.

"Hi!" I waved, walking over.

"Good to see you!" said Rhodri, getting to his feet. "How've you been?"

I shrugged, "Good — crazy, but good. What's new around here?"

Roxie grinned and pointed at her shirt. "I got into the merchandise game for the race. Want a Zipper shirt?"

"No thanks," I said. "I'm actually here to enter myself."

The trio goggled at me. "For real?"

I smiled. "For real."

Exploding into excited chatter, the two men started giving racing advice. Rhodri suggested we should take the classic Carmine Route, while Buzz wanted us to go flat-out and risk the nebula. It quickly turned into an argument. Roxie held back, eyeing me contemplatively. After a minute of patiently waiting for the bickering to stop, she gave up and started talking over the top of the men. "Hey Cassy, do you have a merchandiser?"

I shook my head. "I don't even know what that is."

She grinned, "It's someone who handles your merchandise. I could get some stuff printed up tonight. I know a good bobble head guy."

"For real?" I asked, surprised. "I mean, yeah!"

Roxie laughed. "You didn't even negotiate. You must be very focused on the race."

"Well, I'm not exactly famous. It hadn't occurred to me to make *Erebus* merch. Who would buy it?"

"Let me worry about that."

"What's the standard cut for the racer?"

"20%," she replied casually.

I had a feeling I was being lowballed and despite my hurry I couldn't help but argue, "40%!"

"There she is," said Roxie with a laugh. "30% then. You won't do better than that."

"Deal."

"Excellent," said Roxie, beaming. "I'll get the family to work. My son designed this shirt, you know."

"Really?" I gave it another look. "Hey, he's pretty talented! I better get going, but it was nice to see you."

With a wave to the group, I headed off.

It didn't take long to locate sign-ups, situated as they were in the middle of the large, central atrium.

"Hi," I said, approaching a man wearing a headwrap with the logo of the Diomedes in a repeating pattern. He was sitting behind a counter under a large banner reading, "THE RACE IS ON! Sign-up here" and a timer counting down until the race. 34 minutes remained. The atrium itself was crowded, but the registration table was otherwise empty. The man was watching something on a small datapad and didn't react to my greeting. I tried again.

"I'm here to sign up."

He looked up at me, skeptical. "Do you have the buy-in? Cutting it a bit close, don't you think?"

I fished the buk pouch out of my bra and handed it to him.

He dumped the buks into an authenticator and waited for the results, then nodded. "Looks to be in order." He pulled up a screen on the surface of the desk and started entering information. "Your name?"

"Cassy."

"Home port?"

"Res4, Aavikko."

"Ship's name?"

"*Erebus.*"

He looked up, brow creasing, "Air-bus?"

"No! *Erebus.* E-r-e-b-u-s. You know, it's Greek."

Shrugging, he entered the name, then asked a few more questions about me and my crew.

It was over in less than a minute. The man waved me away impatiently as another latecomer ran up panting behind me, making excuses for being late and fumbling with her purse. Feeling slightly let down at the anticlimax, I started back to the ship, weaving my way through the colorful crowd.

Judging solely on appearances, I guessed a lot of people were here from Sectors 1 and 2, or at least Sector 3 Prime, which was basically Sector 2 anyway. They seemed generally taller than the people from the 3Out, with straight white teeth and smooth skin. They ranged from light skin to dark, short to tall, naturally hued to slightly enhanced to completely artificial. Some were heavily augmented with technology and art, while others looked completely unmodified, even with cosmetics. But they were all strangely good looking, with the look of excellent health that was rare in the 3Out.

A familiar voice sounded to my right, catching my attention. I turned to see Zipper Fanshee and Olivia Winkworth chatting animatedly next to a potted fern.

"Oh!" I said in surprise, staring at them. Zipper was wearing his trademark red bandleader's jacket, gold buttons shining. Olivia stood beside him in a simple yellow jumpsuit and matching heels that set off her ebony skin. I was surprised to see she was several inches taller than him, even without help from the shoes.

Zipper noticed me staring. He gave me a generic smile, then paused, squinting. "Hey!" he said, cocking his head to one side in recognition, "I remember you. You were at the club the other week."

Olivia raised an eyebrow at him.

"What?" said Zipper. "I go to clubs. I'm very popular and cool."

She rolled her eyes. They were dramatically shadowed with a rainbow of blues, greens, reds, and purples.

"I like your make-up," I said.

"Thanks," she said. "Didn't I see you at sign-ups a minute ago? Are you racing?"

"Yup," I said.

Zipper looked at me in surprise, "*You* are racing? In the Diomedes?"

"Yeah?"

"Spicy!" he said, a huge smile crossing his face. "Another 3Out competitor? That's really something! What model is your ship?"

"I think you mean MY ship," a familiar voice said behind me.

I jumped and spun around.

Mal was standing right there.

"Hello, Cassy."

My heart dropped.

Mal's gaze shifted to over my shoulder, "Ah, I see all the trash has collected together. I should have known you 3Outers all knew each other."

"Hi Mal," said Olivia, her voice sugary sweet, "It's been a while."

He gave her a disdainful look. "Oh, hi *Lucus*. I didn't recognize you."

"*Her* name is Olivia," said Zipper, taking a step forward.

"Don't let him push your buttons," said Olivia calmly. "Sticks and stones."

"Oh yes, Velcroboy or whatever your name is. I see you are also playing dress-up," Mal said with a sneer, turning to Zipper and looking him up and down.

"You know what they say," Zipper responded coolly, giving his bandleader's jacket a tug. "Dress for the job you want." He turned to Olivia. "Sign-up time. Will you accompany me?" he proffered an elbow.

She took his arm with a sideways look at Mal and the two walked off, Zipper giving his pompadour a dismissive flick in our direction.

Mal turned to me. "I thought that would get us some privacy."

"Classy," I said.

"You," he said, sticking a finger in my face, "are starting to really piss me off."

"Only just starting? Do I need to try harder?"

He took a menacing step towards me. Kven appeared from nowhere, moving into position behind him, cutting off my escape.

"You better be careful," I said, looking up at him. "You don't want to do anything that will get you banned from Chiba. They don't take kindly to grown men beating up girls in the middle of a public square. And if you get banned from Chiba, you won't be able to sign-up for the Diomedes ever again." I grinned cheekily. Despite everything, I was having fun. "You won't be able to creep on people at the club." I diverted my gaze to somewhere over his right shoulder. "Hey look, a security officer. Officer! Officer!"

Several different emotions chased themselves across Mal's face. Then, with apparent effort, he relaxed, waving off Kven and taking a step back.

"Let's try this again," he said, his voice low and artificially pleasant. "How about we all calm down. There's no reason to get emotional."

"Uh huh," I said.

"If you just think about this rationally, I'm sure you can see that you've painted yourself into a corner. I'm willing to let you go, unharmed, with a promise not to issue a bounty on you or in any way interfere with your life, as long as you give me the AI."

"Hard no," I said. "Cute offer though. Excuse me, I have a race to win."

Slipping between Mal and Kven, I hurried towards the docking bays, half expecting Mal to physically stop me. He didn't, or at least if he tried, he missed, but I could hear him yelling furiously behind me, "Give me back my things, you filthy sand-eater!"

Whatever. I was getting used to the sand-eater thing.

I needed to get back to the ship, but it seemed foolish to head straight there if Mal was following me. Everyone said Chiba security would keep him from doing anything on the station, but I wasn't so sure about that, despite my bravado. After all, security hadn't kept me very safe at the Nibiru Club.

I looked back at the clock. 23 minutes.

Ducking into a large emporium, I weaved between the shoppers, hurrying behind racks of clothes and shoes. I was pretty sure there was a second exit on the far side, near the pneumatic tube to my docking bay. After several minutes of hiding behind displays, pretending to be interested in eyebrow wax, I headed for the far exit, praying my memory was correct.

It was. The transport system was just visible beyond the door.

I exited the shop and was about to hop into the tube when a female voice called out to me, "Hey!"

Startled, I turned to see Olivia hurrying towards me. "I'm glad I caught you," she said. "I want to talk while Zipper takes interviews."

"Sure, but I do have to hurry..." I looked over her shoulder at the distant sign-up banner. 17 minutes.

"I know, I need to hurry too," she said. "But the rumor-mill is going crazy. Word is, you have Mal's racing ship. The one he's been bragging about for years. Is that true?"

"Yup."

Olivia grinned. "Excellent. The enemy of my enemy is my friend, you know? Don't be surprised if you have a lot of supporters. Mal's screwed a bunch of people in his quest to win this race."

"Doesn't seem to have done him much good," I said.

"That's what I wanted to tell you," she said. "He just signed up."

"What!?" I squawked. "How?" My mind was spinning. "He can't possibly race in a Falcon. It's not a racing ship. Not even Captain Ace did that, and he's fictional!"

"Of course not. I don't know if he bought it, borrowed it, or stole it, but he managed to get his hands on a Phantom R-6000."

I blinked. "A Phantom R-6000? Isn't that the same model that won the last race?"

Olivia nodded. "Rumor has it, it's the same *ship* that won the last race. That's why the Abecassis twins aren't defending their title. I hope you have an ace up your sleeve."

"Thanks for letting me know," I said, dazed.

"Good luck," she said, clasping me on the shoulder, then turned and hurried towards the press box.

I watched her go, my head reeling. Mal was still racing?

As if reading my thoughts, Mal entered my line of vision, rounding the far corner of the emporium. Our eyes met. He paused mid-step, then did a heel-turn in my direction, walking directly towards me, his thin lips pressed into a determined line.

Crap.

Suddenly, he jerked to a stop, eyes widening in surprise. Kven had grabbed his arm. Mal turned, slapping the other man's hand away. The two started arguing, faces inches apart, spit flying.

Slowly, I backed towards the transport tube. Neither man noticed me, their attention completely absorbed by the shouting match. Kven was gesturing wildly as Mal shook a finger in his face. I couldn't make out what they were saying, but Kven looked like he was about to call it quits. Mal looked simply murderous.

With a shrug, I turned and jumped into the tube, letting the cool air carry me to safety.

CHAPTER 18
STARTING GUN

I made it back to the *Erebus* as a familiar voice blared over the loudspeakers, ***"Contestants, take your positions on the starting line!"***

I ran into the cockpit to find Una and Joren already seated. Joren started to get up, but I waved him down. "Whose voice was that? I know I've heard it before."

Una pointed to the small screen in the dashboard. It was tuned into the main feed. "It's Perk Hamlin. He's commentating."

"Captain Ace!" I grinned and leaned towards the screen, which had switched from a long-shot of the starting formation to a close-up of a handsome middle-aged man in dark blue robes.

"It is him!" I said. "Although he looks older than I expected."

"I think he looks pretty good for 103," said Una.

"103?" I yelped, looking at her in surprise.

"That's Sector 1 people for you," she said. "Crazy, right?"

"We need to hurry," Pilot interrupted impatiently, his metallic voice excited. Without waiting for a reply, he lifted us out of the docking bay and into the parade of ships moving out of the station. We

took our spot in the starting formation, an enormous block 100 ships high facing the nebula. Behind them, a wall of spectator ships were crowded wing-to-wing, watching eagerly from the sidelines.

"Whoa," said Joren. "That's a lot of people."

"Not just people," said Una, pointing at the ship taking position above us. It was a spherical ship that appeared to be full of water, with dim shapes swimming around inside.

"Dolphins," clarified Una, noting my confusion. "I heard they were entering a ship."

I stared. You didn't normally see tier 1 mammals beside primates this far out, especially not aquatic mammals. They had their own places to live, and it was dangerous for them in the 3Out, with cannibals and all.

"Look," said Joren, pointing. "The ship with the #1 on the side — it's the Abecassis twins!"

"Oh," I said, "about that. I was meaning to tell you. That's Mal. He somehow got their ship. He's flying it himself."

"*WHAT?!*" yelled Una and Pilot in unison.

"Don't worry about it now," I said. "Let's just focus on having a good start." I folded down the small jump-seat behind Una and fastened myself in.

Several colorful ships wove past us, quickly moving into place farther down the formation, solar panels glinting down their rainbow sides.

Perk Hamlin's voice came over the speakers again, his craggy face grinning from the screen in the dash, *"Ladies, Gentleman, In-Betweens, Neithers, and tier 1 mammals of all descriptions — Welcome!"*

He paused as a roar from the crowd on the station almost blew out the speakers. When the cheering died down, he continued, *"I welcome you all to the Diomedes 100! This, our 163th running, is an extra special event, as it marks the first time we've had over 2,000 competitors on the field! To mark the occasion, our gracious sponsor, Fin's Gin and Pharmaceuticals, has increased this year's first place prize to an historic record of TWO million buks!"*

Joren gasped. Una shushed him.

"Who will that lucky winner be? Only time will tell. They could be from anywhere, as our brave challengers represent 81 separate planets and colonies, seven different species, and all three sectors!"

He paused for cheering, then continued, his voice low with excitement. *"And now, without further ado, the moment you've all been waiting for..."* he pulled the starting gun from his robes and held it in the air, *"On the count of 5...4...3...2...1..."*

He pulled the trigger.

"GO!" He yelled in thunderous unison with the crowd on Hub Chiba.

There was a moment of stillness, and then all hell broke free.

Somewhere to our right, there was an enormous explosion. It rocked the *Erebus*, slamming me painfully against the restraints. On the dash screen, the main feed showed a collision as two racers jumped into each other, the space around them erupting in a white ball of flame.

Pilot moved us sharply away, heading towards open space. We were almost out of the starting grid when another ship flew past us, meters from colliding. I got a glimpse of a jagged looking silver ship with "*Shango's Axe*" painted on the side as it spun by.

"We need to move!" I urged.

"No kidding," said Pilot, but he swooped to starboard and started gaining speed. *"Hold on."*

I gripped the bottom of my seat and held on.

We exited the jump at the mouth of the nebula. The field had spread out a bit, but even so, hundreds of ships were exiting their initial jump far too close for comfort.

"Whoa!" said Joren as another ship flashed into view meters from us.

Pilot swerved again, throwing me against my restraints as we zipped away from the main artery of the race and towards the opaque nebula that swirled beneath us.

"Look!" said Una, pointing at the viewscreen.

A ship sparkled brightly in the distance, throwing off beams of rainbow light in all directions.

"It's *Starlight Express*!" I said, recognizing it from the last race. "And look, more veterans! I think that's *Pertinax's Revenge*!"

We all craned our necks to look at the huge black ship moving smoothly along the standard racing line, smaller ships zipping around it like colorful, flashing minnows.

"Wow," I marveled.

"Sorry to interrupt the fan tour, but it's nebula time," whooped Pilot.

With what sounded suspiciously like a *"weeeeeee,"* he angled us away from the main group and slid into the first layer of nebula, purple gasses whispering across the viewscreen.

The nebula was a death sentence for most ships, even this first, thin layer. We would be alone now.

Two ships followed us in.

Oh.

"Look! Forget *Pertinax*, LOOK! It's Bixby Thorne!" cried Joren.

"Isn't he dead?" I asked, following Joren's gaze.

"Guess not," he said. "That's definitely his green ship. He was my favorite as a kid."

Bixby Thorne was Diomedes Royalty. He won the 2392 race in a smoking escape pod after his racing ship was destroyed by a rogue gravity ribbon. A lot of old-timers still said it was the best race ever.

His ship was keeping pace with us at a near distance, following our swoops and swirls, matching us move for move...

In the blink of an eye, the green ship jerked to one side and slammed into an asteroid, as if swatted by a giant hand. Debris flew in all directions, painting colorful streaks in the bright nebula gasses.

Speaking of rogue gravity ribbons…

"Yikes," I said.

"Was that Bixby?" Una asked, nervously.

"Hope not..." Joren said, eyes wide.

"Hold on," said Pilot. *"We are going deeper."*

The second ship faded as the screen turned solid purple, the nebula completely obscuring our view.

"That's it," said Una after a few minutes. "We've lost long range sensors and communications. There won't be any more race updates until we cross the main route again. We're completely alone."

Joren sighed, slumping back in the command chair. "Phhewww! Now *that* was exciting!"

"Pilot," I asked, unbuckling my restraints and straightening up, "Is there anything you need from us?"

There was silence. "Gotcha," I responded. "We'll let you concentrate."

"Maybe you and Joren should run maintenance checks," suggested Una. "Make sure the jump drive didn't get rattled, put some more kakorine in the engine, that kind of stuff. I'm going to run scenarios with Pilot.

"No, you aren't," responded Pilot.

"Yes, I am!" said Una indignantly.

"You know, Una," I said, slowly backing up. "You're right. Joren and I will run some system checks, and you should help us."

"Maybe later," she said, her back to me, hands flying across the controls.

I rolled my eyes but didn't argue.

"Everything looks okay," said Joren a few minutes later, looking around the engine room. "I'm not sure what to do."

"Just keep the toolbox handy. And get ready to feed the engine kakorine as needed," I said. "But honestly, Pilot is in charge now."

"Tell that to Una," said Joren.

I didn't need to. A few minutes later, Una huffed into the engine room. She looked at me with irritation as if deciding what to say, then sighed. "I guess I'll be in the mess hall. Do you like cookies?"

Without waiting for either of us to respond, she turned and walked away.

Joren and I looked at each other and shrugged.

An hour later she reappeared with a plate of mock-choc and dried currant...blobs. She watched us with an expectant air as we each took a nibble.

"Yum!" I said. They were okay. Very...sticky.

Joren nodded and tried to say something, but his mouth was stuck shut. "Mppffff!" He gave a thumbs up instead.

Una nodded, then disappeared back into the mess hall.

I finished my cookie but didn't grab another.

It was later that evening before I heard from Pilot again. He crackled over the loudspeakers while I was helping Joren clean up from dinner.

"Captain."

I almost dropped a plate. "Yikes!" I juggled it for a moment before catching it and putting it back in the cabinet. "What is it?"

"We have re-entered the primary race route and have reestablished network communications. The Erebus is flying in 210th position."

There was a crash behind me as a glass fell to the floor. "210th?" Joren said excitedly, a smile lighting his face, "After just one shortcut? Oh, this is going to work." He bent down and picked up the glass, which had bounced harmlessly. Everything on this ship was designed to be thrown around.

"That's great," I said. "Let me know if I can help, okay?"

"Keep her off me," he said.

"Roger," I replied.

Una burst into the room, vibrating with energy. "Did you hear?! We are doing so well! Pilot, can I—"

"Hey Una," I interrupted. "Pilot is busy. I think we meatsacks should get some rest while we can. Who knows what will happen tomorrow."

Una nodded, twitching like a nervous rabbit. "Good idea, but there is no way I'm going to be able to sleep. I'll bake some more cookies."

I started to say that wasn't necessary, but reconsidered after seeing the look on her face. "Yum!" I said instead, forcing a grin. "More cookies!"

Joren and I were sitting on the floor of the lounge, our backs to the wall, flicking playing cards across the bay. Una had left the cards out for us, but we didn't know any games. I didn't even recognize all of the symbols.

"I win again," muttered Joren as his card bounced off the far wall and into the box we had set up as a goal. "Yay."

"Pilot?" I asked the ceiling, "Can we have a status update, please?"

There was a fraction of a pause, then Pilot responded, *"I'm busy."*

I narrowed my eyes, "That's an order."

I could almost hear the AI roll his eyes before responding, *"Aye aye, Captain. We are currently deep within the nebula, but as of the last sensor readings, we are in 23rd place."*

Joren and I exchanged excited looks, "We are in the money?!"

"For now," Pilot responded. *"But as I've said many times, our strategy relies on complex nebula navigation, not speed, so shut up and let me concentrate."*

Joren and I mimed zipping our lips, then grinned.

"You know?" said Joren. "This might actually work."

"Right?"

Una stuck her head into the lounge. "Hey you guys, I'm going to make cookies! Any requests?"

We both groaned.

Una stiffened, looking hurt. "What kind of reaction is that? I'm baking for *you*!"

"Una," I said. "You are baking because you are stressed. We can't eat this many cookies. The freezer is full and the food waste is making me anxious."

She glared at me, then sighed, her shoulder slumping. "Fine. I guess I'll paint instead."

"Nah, come hang out," said Joren. "I barely know you."

"Yeah!" I agreed excitedly. "Hang out! We can play a game."

Una brightened. "A card game? Okay! What do you want to play? Rummy? Skat? Martian baccarat?"

Joren looked at her with amusement. "Umm…maybe not a card game. Do you know anything simpler? Maybe a drinking game?"

Una looked startled, "A drinking game? Do we even have anything to drink? Wait, I know the answer to that. Give me a minute."

She disappeared, reappearing a moment later holding a bottle of wine and three glasses. "Mal bought this to celebrate his win. It's probably really nice." She peered at the label.

"I'm sure it's wasted on us, but break it out!" grinned Joren.

"If we are trying to get to know each other," Una said as she unscrewed the top, "how about we play 'Not Me'?"

Joren and I looked at her blankly.

"It's easy," she said, taking a seat on the couch and crossing her legs. Joren and I crawled off the floor and took a seat on either side of her. She handed us each a glass and divided the wine equally. It was a deep purple blue and glowed in the soft light of the lounge.

"I learned this game at summer camp."

"Summer camp?"

"Yeah, you know, a place in the forest you do sports and activities."

That sounded vaguely familiar. I had seen a horror holo that took place at a summer camp. The swim instructor killed all the campers and made a submarine out of their flayed skins. It was weird. "Did you like it?" I asked, cautiously.

"Of course! The camps on Zopyros IX are the best. Half the planet is covered in dense forests with trees that are perfect for climbing, and the other half is a huge warm ocean. It has slightly higher gravity than Earth-standard, so it's very popular for workout camps.

"Workout camps? Wait, were you sent to a fat camp?" Joren grinned. "Like Bash Blitzen in the Captain Ace flashback special?"

"No! And you aren't supposed to call them that." She paused. "The camp next to us was an adiposally inclined though, and they always beat us in tug-of-war. It was really unfair."

I giggled, "So, how does this drinking game work?"

Una gave the wine label a final look, screwed the lid back on, and set the bottle down. "The person in charge says "This person has" or "This person has not," and then everyone else has to answer "Me" or "Not Me." If you say, "Me", you drink. That's about it. If you are the one asking, your answer needs to be "Not Me," so don't say stuff you've done."

"Sounds easy enough. Pilot, do you want to play?" I asked the air.

"Play a drinking game with teenagers? I would love to," he responded flatly.

"Really?"

"No."

"Oh."

"What kind of questions?" asked Joren.

"Silly stuff, just to get to know each other," Una answered. "Like, I could say, 'This person has never been to summer camp.'"

Joren and I both rolled our eyes and said, "Me" in unison.

Una nodded. "That's it. Or, my go-to, 'This person has *never* skipped a class.'"

Joren and I stared at her. "What, like going AWOL from a training day?"

"Sure," said Una.

Joren shook his head. "Not me."

"I wouldn't have dared pull anything like that," I said. "The Company would have fined me."

"Oh." Una looked disappointed. "That one usually works."

"So, we are trying to get each other to drink. I get it," said Joren. "Okay, let's start for real. I'll go. This person has…" he eyed Una, "…never broken a bone."

"Not me," I said.

"Me," said Una. "Seriously? What bones have you broken? That's so medieval."

"It's not evil, it's normal," I responded. "I've broken my foot a couple times, but the worst was my arm. That took weeks to heal. My shifts were so painful."

"Remember when I broke my leg?" asked Joren. "It was so bad I was put on monitor duty. If Bihn hadn't paid to get me an upgraded cast I would've been crippled. That was a great cast though. Healed it up in few days."

Una grimaced and took a sip.

"Okay, my turn," I said, also eyeing her speculatively. "This person…has never gone 24 hours without a shower."

Una took another sip, then said, slightly coolly, "It's not nice to target people. My turn. This person…um…has gone streaking."

Joren took a big sip.

"What?" I laughed. "When?"

"Maybe you shouldn't have skipped all the after-work parties." He winked at me. "My turn. This person has peed their pants at work."

"Hey!" I cried, "You know that was because of a gas leak! Everyone on shift peed their pants that night, even Mae!"

Una laughed, "Gross! Not me! You drink, Cassy!"

I took a sip. The wine was thick and sweet, almost spicy, and warmth spread quickly throughout my body. I wiggled my toes happily.

"Your turn," Joren said to me.

I turned to him. "Okay, buddy, you asked for it. This person has a tattoo."

Joren said, "Me" and raised his glass to his lips, but so did Una.

I gaped at her. "Wait, you have a *tattoo*?"

Una nodded, smiling slyly. "I haven't shown you? I got it when I turned 16." She unbuttoned her top and turned to reveal her left shoulder. Etched into her milky white skin was a small black-and-white schematic of the *Caracalla*, the first racing ship to win the Diomedes 100. "Mom let me. She was so cool, always pushing me to do new things. It was one of the last things we did together." Una looked down and cleared her throat.

"That's unexpected," said Joren, peering at her shoulder. "Very cool!"

"Thanks," she said, rebuttoning her top.

"Whose turn is it?" I asked.

"It's mine," said Una. She thought for a second, then dropped her voice as if saying something scandalous, "This person has done silver leaf."

Joren and I looked at each other, shrugged, and drank.

Una looked shocked. "But…it's super dangerous."

I shrugged again. "Not in leaf form. I guess sometimes people chew too much and get the runs. That *is* pretty dangerous."

"Too much information, Cassy," Joren interrupted. "My turn. And for that image, *this* person has stolen from work." He looked at me.

"I returned everything!" I replied indignantly.

"But did you have permission?"

"…no…" I took a sip. Feeling cheeky, I raised an eyebrow at Una and made a guess. "This person has never kissed anyone."

She flushed a bright pink.

"Not me," said Joren.

"Me," said Una in a small voice, then took a sip. Her whole face was red. "I…I'm getting tired. I'm going to go to bed."

"No! Come on, stay here," I said, backpaddling. "Let's watch a holo. Do you have anything?"

She nodded, relaxing back into the couch, "There's some shows saved. Pilot, pull up the Queen Kleopatra holiday special."

"I love that show!" exclaimed Joren. "I didn't know there was a holiday special! What holiday?"

"Hogmanay," said Una.

"Makes sense," I said.

"Not really," said Una. "But that's okay. It's a good episode."

We snuggled down. Joren yawned.

By the time the opening theme song had finished, we were all asleep.

Hours passed.

Days passed.

Outside the windows was a solid purple mass. There were no other ships.

I was sprawled in the lounge, half-heartedly reading the *Erebus'* owner's manual. Joren dozed beside me.

"GUYS!"

Una burst in, the ends of her hair splattered purple with paint. "It's TIME!" she yelled.

Joren jerked in surprise and fell off the couch. I jumped to my feet.

"Dionto's Rings?" I asked.

"Dionto's Rings," she confirmed.

The two of us sprinted to the cockpit, Joren scrabbling behind us.

Dionto's Rings marked the final stretch of the race. The vast majority of racers went around the large star cluster, which took a while but was navigationally simple, allowing for exciting side-by-side racing and other action that could only take place in clean space. But it was also possible to go *behind* the cluster, through a section of the nebula that was relatively thin. Several ships had attempted it over the years but only one, *Bellerophon*, had actually done it. Their jump drive was damaged in the process and they had to limp to the finish line, but with the Dionto shortcut they still managed to grab number 76. Several other ships had attempted the route but none had been heard from again.

Word was, the contents of that region shifted so rapidly that mapping it was pretty much impossible.

Una had done it though. Or at least, she had figured out a path that had a high likelihood of being unobstructed, which was still impressive. With Pilot's flying ability, we were confident it would be a snooze. After all, for the past week we had been successfully navigating much denser parts of the nebula. And once we were through the Rings, it was a single jump to the finish line.

Just one more jump, and we would win.

We rushed into the cockpit, Una and I grabbing the two command chairs while Joren leaned in the doorway, staring over our heads at the swirling gases outside.

"The nebula is getting thinner," he said.

Joren was right. It was noticeably less foggy out the window, and I could start to make out shapes in the distance. As I squinted, a planet slowly swam into view, a large green and brown sphere streaked with white puffy clouds, encircled by a rocky grey ring.

"You know, that's a pretty nice looking planet for being in the nebula," Joren said in surprise, and I was about to agree when a small shape next to the planet caught my eye.

Was that a ship?

"Is that a ship?" asked Una, squinting at the viewscreen.

"Yes," said Pilot, flatly. *"It's a Phantom R-6000."*

"A Phantom R-6000? Oh no, it's Mal!" I yelped.

"What!" Joren craned his neck at the screen. "What's he doing here?"

"I don't know!" I said, my heart racing. "Why risk this shortcut when you have the fastest ship?"

"Oh," said Una, her voice small. "I *may* have told him about my route."

"YOU WHAT?!?" we all shouted in unison.

"I didn't think he was listening to me!" she yelled back. "He never listened to me!"

"Well, he did this time," I said, "But why is he just waiting here?"

As if to answer my question, a large rock from the planet's rings flew out of formation and shot towards us. It zipped by us on the starboard side, narrowly missing the *Erebus* and spinning off into the nebula.

"Whoa!" I cried, surprised.

"Did Mal do that?" asked Joren. "How?"

"I don't know," said Una, sounding confused.

Another rock flew towards us, as if thrown by an invisible hand. It missed us by inches.

"Pilot?" I said, nervously.

Erebus jerked roughly as another projectile, what looked like the wing of a wrecked ship, hurtled towards us, but the sudden movement brought us into contact with an anti-gravity ribbon. Pilot was usually good at avoiding those, but we hit this one hard. It threw us back up into the make-shift weapon, which scraped loudly against the top of the ship.

"Can we get out of here?" I said, gripping the armrests with white knuckles.

"I'm trying," said Pilot, the stress noticeable in his voice.

Something slammed into us from the port side, knocking Joren to his hands and knees. The ship shivered and there was an explosion in the engine room.

"Uh oh..." said Joren, pulling himself upright.

Una stared out the viewscreen, eyes wide, "He's...he's...*trying to kill me!*"

Joren looked at her in confusion, rubbing his knee, "You already knew Mal was a killer. He tried to kill Cassy."

"That's not the same!"

A speeder-sized rock flew straight at us, bouncing off the viewscreen with a resounding "CLUNK."

"This is bad," Una said, momentarily distracted as her hands flew over the controls. "We can't keep this up for long."

Pilot broke in, *"Our thruster control cable is broken. It needs to be repaired before we can take evasive maneuvers."*

"On it," said Joren. "Give me a minute." He disappeared down the hallway.

Another rock flew past us, narrowly missing the viewscreen. The next shot grazed our port wing.

"Joren needs to hurry," Pilot said nervously.

"Umm..." I said, pointing at the screen. "I have bad news."

The bloated corpse of a huge derelict ship was hurtling towards us.

"Shit!" Una yelled. "We need to move! NOW"

"Thrusters are still offline!" cried Pilot, his metallic voice modulating wildly. *"So are weapons!"*

"Distress call?" I barked, heart racing.

"Sent!"

I heard Joren's distant voice pleading for time, but there wasn't any.

It was going to hit us.

In a flash, a bright yellow racer burst out of a jump, positioning itself defensibly between us and the incoming wreck. They opened fire. The derelict ship exploded into two pieces, flying harmlessly past us on either side.

The newcomer waved a wing at us.

It was Zipper Fanshee.

"Zipper!" I cried.

Una looked over her shoulder in surprise. "You know Zipper Fanshee?"

"Sort of!" I said, excitedly. "Oh, this is fantastic. He's helping us!"

It was Zipper's distinctive yellow ship all right, built for maneuverability with two short wings and a tall stabilizing fin, the number 64 emblazoned in black across the side. I was surprised the small ship had so much firepower, but I wasn't about to complain.

"Try now!" came Joren's voice from the engine room.

"Pilot, let's move!" I yelled.

"I'm working on it!" he yelled back.

The *Erebus* tipped to one side, swinging around and heading back into the dense gasses. We just needed to get out of visual range. Mal couldn't follow us into the nebula. Although neither could Zipper...

A large blast flashed outside, brightly illuminating the cockpit.

Zipper's ship exploded.

To my left, I could see Una's pale face light in horror as the yellow ship blew apart, spewing smoke and flames in all directions.

"Zipper! NO!"

The large yellow fin was flying towards us.

It was coming fast.

Erebus dodged, turning her nose down and diving like a falcon.

We weren't fast enough.

Erebus rocked from a violent explosion in the stern. The lights flickered and half the cockpit controls went dark.

"NO!" shouted Joren from the engine room. "Damn it!

"*Captain,*" said Pilot, "*There is a fire in the aft control panel and the fire suppression systems are unresponsive. We are in immediate danger of losing life support.*"

"On it!" I yelled, jumping up and sprinting down the hallway, pausing only to smash my fist into an emergency panel to grab a small metal canister marked 'FIRE.' Black smoke poured from the stern starboard corridor. I hit it with the extinguisher and the cloud flickered briefly, then sprang back, angered. The fire was coming from inside a panel, and from this angle I wasn't reaching it. Dropping to my knees, I scrambled around the plume of smoke and hunkered down by the escape pod launch controls. From here I could see the root of the fire, a knot of flames consuming what used to be some type of circuit breaker. I hit it with the extinguisher.

BOOMMM! the entire panel exploded, blowing me back against the far wall, stars exploding in my head. For a confused second I stared at the fire extinguisher still gripped in my hand, sweat dripping down my face, wondering what just happened.

"*Captain!*" Pilot shouted from a speaker above me, "*We've been hit! Structural integrity is failing!*"

"No!" I struggled to my feet, choking on the smoke. The heat was ripping at my skin, keeping me from retreating to the cockpit. "NO!"

"*GET IN THE ESCAPE POD!*" Pilot yelled.

There was another explosion to my right, knocking me back to the ground. The fire rose in a wall in front of me, behind me, beside me. There was a sound of tearing metal. The ship was falling apart.

"*GO!*" Pilot screamed.

I scrambled forward, outstretched hand slamming against the emergency controls.

The hatch sprung open and I dove in headfirst, hot air encircling my body. Flames chasing me into the tiny pod, fiery hands grabbing at my legs.

And then it was dark and cold.

There was a moment of silence as I lay in a crumpled ball. A screen in front of me lit with a number.

"3" it read.

"2" came next.

"1" it flashed, and with a shudder, the escape pod flew into open space.

I had left the *Erebus*.

CHAPTER 21
ALONE

The escape pod spun towards the planet. I was thrown around like a rock in a tumbler, head over heels, smashing into walls, my nose crunching. After a few spins I caught a handle near the hatch and held on for dear life.

Through the hatch's window I could see a cascade of debris swirling around me, yellow fragments turning red, then black, disintegrating into nothing.

Yellow fragments. Zipper's ship.

The spin of the pod slowed, stabilizers automatically kicking in. I caught a glimpse of a black ship flying away, the #1 one of the side gleaming, unharmed.

There were no other escape pods.

And then the window outside went dark as the pod shook violently. A fiery ball of light appeared above me, growing larger as it turned from orange to red to magenta, then back to orange, and then yellow as we punched through the atmosphere and daylight flooded through the small window. The pod gave another jerk and a red striped parachute opened above me, catching the pod and carrying it gently to rest.

CRUNCH.

The pod slammed into the ground, skidded a few meters, then came to a halt. Through the hatch above me I could see a pink sky filled with fluffy white clouds.

I let myself drop the few feet to the pod floor. My hands were cramped in the shape of the handle and I took a minute to stretch them out, then spent another minute checking over the rest of my body. Everything seemed to be fine, with the exception of my nose, which was definitely broken. Gritting my teeth, I popped it back into place, then let myself scream in pain. There was no one here to hear me. I screamed louder.

That felt better. I screamed one more time, less out of pain and more out of panic and frustration. The scream echoed around the pod, sounding thin and scared.

Well, I was scared.

There was a small computer panel to my right and I hit some buttons, but it was damaged and only gave limited readings. I soon gave up.

Not sure what else to do, I climbed up to the hatch and hit the open button. There was a pause as the pod tested the atmosphere, then the door slid open with a soft POP. A rush of clean air filled the chamber. I took a deep breath. It tasted a bit weird, with an off-flavor that reminded me of the mine, but otherwise seemed okay.

I stuck out my head.

I was in a rocky ravine, looking up at the side of a shale-covered hill. I could see nothing but multicolored rocks and the rosy sky above, the white clouds almost cartoonishly full and wooly.

I crawled out of the pod, landing lightly on the shale-covered ground. The air was surprisingly warm and slightly humid. I unzipped my jumpsuit halfway and tied the arms around my waist.

There were no signs of ships.

No signs of life.

I'm the only survivor. I killed all my friends. This is all my fault.

Don't think about that! Start climbing. There must be something at the top of this hill.

I started to climb.

The shale was hard to grip and I was soon on all fours, scrambling up the side of the hill like a weasel. It was exhausting work, and by the time I reached the top of the crest I was covered in sweat and panting.

There was nothing there.

Just another hill.

I turned around. I could see for miles behind me, and beside my crashed pod there was nothing but rocks and ravines. It was just like the Aavikko wastelands. Nothing.

I wasn't sure what I had been expecting. It's not like there would be a settlement here in the nebula. I was lucky this planet even had an atmosphere.

Lucky.

Lucky.

If it wasn't for me, there was a good chance Joren would be safe on Aavikko, not running off with raiders to chase me across the sector. Una would still be on-board the *Chaos*, watching the race from the comfort of her own room.

Zipper would be on his way to a win.

He must have been very close when Mal attacked, visual range even. That was the only way to risk a jump without full sensor data. It was the jump he was saving to get to the finish line, but he burned it on a tiny hop just to save me.

What a waste.

At least I was somewhat helpful to Pilot.

Who was also dead. Totally and completely. And that was the best-case scenario, because if he was still functional, Mal was going to retrieve him and deliver him to the Oberion League.

And the Oberion League would wipe out the rebellion.

And the children of the 3Out would remain slaves.

And I wouldn't even know because I'd be dead, alone, on this unnamed, lousy planet.

Lucky.

I laid down in the rocks and cried.

There was smoke coming from over the hill.

It drifted lazily over the top of the rainbow shale, so faint that at first I didn't trust my eyes.

No, that was definitely smoke.

I pulled myself to my feet, rocks cascading down the hill behind me, bouncing off the escape pod with a distant *TINK-TINK-TINK*. My hands were screaming from the hundreds of small cuts I had collected on the scrabble up, and with the adrenaline wearing off, the bruises from the crash landing were starting to complain.

I forced myself upward. It was just as hard as before, and this hill was much larger, but the *smoke*.

I thought about what I would find, and then immediately regretted it. There would be corpses. Burnt, mutilated corpses, like the bodies pulled out of the mine after hitting a methane vein.

What I really needed was to find Pilot, and fast. He was the important one. At least I could run off with his program and hide from Mal and the League in the desert until I died.

Great plan, Cassy.

Hey, at least it's something.

The hill seemed to grow as I climbed. Looking back, I could see to the horizon, the lip of the planet's rings barely visible in the distance.

I was almost at the top of the hill.

Five steps forward, one slip back, three more forward, and I pulled myself, teeth gritted, muscles trembling, onto the crest of the ridge.

There was a beat as I caught my breath. Then I looked down and gasped.

Below me was the *Erebus*.

I blinked and looked again.

It was certainly the *Erebus*. The ship looked completely intact, bright red and gleaming, a few light scratches barely visible on the smooth armor plating.

What?

My eyes sought the smoke.

It was coming from the charred, twisted, blackened wreckage *next* to the *Erebus*.

Zipper's ship lay in two large chunks, with smaller debris littered across the narrow valley. The largest section was smoking heavily, sending thick, black plumes shooting into the pink sky.

There were three little figures standing next to the wreckage.

One of them pointed in my direction, then the other two turned and waved.

I waved back, dazed.

What?

Without another thought I started running down the hill towards them, slipping and sliding down the loose rocks. I tripped and stumbled at the foot of the slope, running headlong into Joren.

"Ooof!"

He caught me and swung me around, laughing. "Cassy! You okay?"

I took a step back and nodded. "Are you?"

He nodded back, his face lit by an enormous grin, "We're all fine!"

Una and Zipper ran up.

"It took you long enough," teased Una. "I was starting to think we would have the ship fixed by the time you got here."

"It's fixable?" I asked, amazed.

Una nodded, "Yes. The damage is all pretty minor, considering. We should have it repaired in a day or so. It was mostly our life support and thruster controls that were hit, which sounds bad, but Joren's already repaired the thruster control cord, and the life support was the only thing that wasn't fried on Zipper's ship, so we are using those parts to repair. We've already moved the relevant wreckage to the *Erebus'* engine room. The weapon system totally destroyed, but we can fly without it."

"That's wonderful," I said, scratching my head, then turned to Zipper, "How did *you* survive?"

"Cockpit escape pod." He gestured at the nose of his ship, which was blackened but mostly intact.

A cockpit escape pod, like on the *Erebus A*. Of course.

"You *are* okay, right?" Joren asked again. "We were going to send out a rescue team, but we wanted to move the life control stuff from Zipper's ship before it caught fire again. Pilot said you would be fine. He tracked your pod to the other side of the hill. The onboard computer showed you our location, right?"

"No," I said. "It was damaged."

Suddenly, I felt foolish. While I had been lamenting the death of my friends and crying my face off, they were fixing the ship and calmly waiting for me to rejoin them.

"Your face is covered in blood," observed Una.

"I'm fine," I said again.

Something had been bothering me since we reunited.

"Umm," I said, "This might be a weird question, but is everyone's voice just a little higher pitched than normal? Are my ears broken?"

Joren laughed. It was definitely *not* his normal, deep chuckle.

"It's the helium," Una said. "There's more in the atmosphere than Earth-standard. I think this planet has an extra-radioactive crust." Now that I was listening for it, she sounded a lot like a cartoon chipmunk.

"Great," I said, then laughed, the high-pitched giggles bouncing around the valley. "At least I'm not going crazy. How long have we been separated, anyway?"

Zipper glanced down at the small computer built into his wrist, "It's been about 45 minutes."

"Oh," I said, feeling even more foolish. "I thought it had been longer than that."

Suddenly, I was hit by a huge wave of relief. It was nice I didn't have do everything by myself. "Good job, crew," I said. "Really good job."

Curious to see the damage, I walked to the *Erebus* and entered through the airlock.

The hallway was black.

I blinked and looked again. The formerly white hallway was charred, the walls deformed and covered in hard, black bubbles. The floor was melted away to reveal patches of black grating. The interior doors must have sealed shut before the explosion, I thought, as I could see the engine room, storage room, and cockpit were clean and untouched.

I would have been burnt to a crisp.

"Thank you, Pilot," I said. "I wouldn't have gotten in the escape pod if you hadn't made me."

"You're welcome, Captain," said Pilot.

"Heads up!" said Una, throwing me an ice pack. "You should probably wash your face. And your hands. And just...everything.

Actually, we should all disinfect once we leave this place. Who knows what we've picked up."

"Great," I said, but went and took a shower.

Sometime later, clean and clothed in my green jumpsuit, I wandered into the engine room to find Zipper swapping out a power regulator. He had changed out of his bandleader's jacket and was wearing a simple blue tunic over his racing leggings. Una was sitting in the corner, plugged into the veb, listening to something while welding a circuit board with a soldering iron. I sat down next to Zipper. "Can I help?"

He gestured at a panel on the engine, "You can take off that panel. I need to get in there next."

I pulled out my hairpin and got to work on the screws. He watched me with interest, possibly about to recommend a screwdriver, but once I got the first screw out he shrugged and went back to work.

After several hours of helping Zipper with repairs, I asked the question that had been pestering me since the crash. "Zipper, why did you help us? Really? I mean, this is a *race*."

Zipper rolled his sleeves to his elbows and stuck his arm deep into the kakorine feeding tube, "Anyone from 3Out who gets anywhere does so because they fought for it. We have to support each other. It's not a big deal, honestly. I'll rebuild the *Tachi-Machi.* Or scrape together the buks for a new ship. Worst case scenario, I'll go back to the Tour de Cymbeline and win some prize money there. Anyway, like you said, it's a *race*. It's *just* a race. Screw that Mal guy. He's a total shithead."

"He is my dad," said Una quietly from the corner. She had removed the veb connection from her ear.

"Sorry," said Zipper. "Total *poop*-head."

Una lowered her eyes. "Never mind. Call him whatever you want."

"How do you know him?" I asked Zipper.

"Hub Chiba isn't so big," said Zipper. "He and Olivia go way back. But it's not my story to tell."

Joren wandered in, panting and wiping his forehead. "Whew! The welding work on the exterior plating is finished. It will get us back to Hub Chiba at least." He took a seat next to us on the floor. "What was that thing anyway? That weapon that Mal used? It looked like some sort of tractor beam."

"I have no idea," said Zipper. "I've never seen anything like it."

"When I was aboard the Chaos," I said, "I overheard the crew talking about a slingshot. I think that was it."

Zipper let out a low whistle. "A slingshot. It's a good idea, really, if you are a dirty cheater. It's definitely not legal to use on competitors, but it would be hard to prove if we were smashed to smithereens. Even if our wreckage was recovered it would probably look like we ran into something, not that something was rammed into *us*."

Joren nodded, "The only times anyone has been disqualified for cheating was when they used energy weapons. But no one will be looking for our wreckage except for Mal anyway. Oh!" He sat up straight and looked at me. "That reminds me! I was going through the *Erebus A* and I think I found the remains of a tracking device. It looks like it was damaged when the ship blew apart."

"So that's how I was followed to Hub Chiba."

Joren nodded again.

I sighed, "I feel like I've been one step behind this whole time."

"I'm still confused," said Zipper. "If Mal wants your fancy AI, why isn't he here now?"

Una spoke from her spot in the corner, her voice low and resentful, "Knowing him, he's still trying to win the race. His main goal has always been the race. We are one jump from the finish line." She narrowed her eyes. "He wants to win, swing by on the way back to Hub Chiba, loot Pilot from our dead bodies, grab his prize money, then give Pilot to the League before they know anything ever went wrong. Big winner, Malaki Sjöberg." She got to her feet. "We have a little time. He won't be able to jump again immediately. He'll be using impulse speed."

Pilot broke in over the loudspeakers, *"It is likely that Mal is under the impression that the Erebus was destroyed, or at least severely damaged, on impact. The ship took a hard line for the planet to follow the escape pod, and we were heavily smoking from the pod's chute. By the time we landed we were under heavy cloud cover.*

Additionally, Zipper's ship caused an explosion on impact. Mal will expect us to be in fragments."

"That's crazy," said Joren. "If the League was after me, I would grab Pilot first even if it meant not winning."

"Mal doesn't care about anything but the race. Not anything," said Una, bitterly.

I looked at her. "Una, I don't think he knew you were onboard. I'm pretty sure he thinks you caught a transport back to Elea."

She didn't answer.

"Don't worry," I continued, trying to get her to look at me, "We're going to fix this ship and wipe that smug look off Mal's face. We'll cross the finish line!"

"Sure," she said, her eyes puffy. Suddenly, she turned and left the room.

Joren, Zipper, and I looked at each other.

"Is she okay?" asked Joren.

"I have no idea," I replied.

It was at least an hour before she returned, striding into the engine room with her head held high.

Her hair was gone.

Una had shaved her head.

She paused in the doorway, looking both defiant and incredibly self-conscious.

We all stared at her.

"He liked my hair," she said, simply.

Zipper gave her a thumbs up. "Spicy. You have a fortunate head shape."

Her lips twitched cautiously and she rubbed her hand across her bare scalp, "Um, thanks."

"You okay?" I asked.

"Yes," she said.

"Good. You look great." She did too.

Una smiled.

"Crew," said Pilot over the loudspeaker, *"I just completed a system review and we are operational."*

We swiveled our heads to the speaker in unison. "Really?!"

"Yes," said Pilot. *"I will run through the checklists several thousand more times, but prepare to leave in the next ten minutes."*

"Spicy!" said Zipper. "At least we'll get to finish."

"Again, I'm sorry about your race," I said.

"I already said it's fine," said Zipper. "I would have *liked* to win, but I can wait for the next race." He sighed dramatically, "I had already spent that 2 million buk purse though." He tapped the side of his head. "In my mind, at least."

"What were you going to buy?" I asked.

"You first," he replied, cheekily.

"Me?" I said. "With all that money, I could fly this ship for the rest of my life, even if business was bad. I could go anywhere I wanted. And people wouldn't patronize me. Everything would be...I don't know...easier."

Zipper nodded. "A Diomedes number greases the wheels, that's for sure."

"So, what would you buy with a win?" I asked.

"Oh, I would have some fun." He grinned. "I have a shopping list ready. It's mostly custom clothes and shoes from all the hot designers. With a top-notch wardrobe and a #1 on the side of my ship, I'd be the spiciest guy on Chiba. Then I'd pour money into the veb channel I'm starting with Olivia, and probably buy another apartment for the fan club." He turned to Una. "What about you? What do you want the money for?"

Una looked startled, "The money? I hadn't thought about it."

Zipper raised an eyebrow. "You hadn't thought about it?"

She shrugged. "I don't really think about money, not unless I have to."

Zipper shot me a look but didn't say anything.

"I know what I want," said Joren with surprising determination. "A farm."

"What?" I said, turning to him in surprise.

"Yes," said Joren, passionately. "A vegetable farm on a nice, stable, well-managed planet where I can be a member of a functional society."

"Oh," I said, not sure how to respond.

"I'm finished," said Pilot. *"We're ready."*

I got to my feet and faced the crew. "Okay everybody! Great work on the repairs. I'm really, really impressed. It's been 19 hours since the crash, which means we are on day 11 of the race, which means there is a *chance* it isn't over yet. Why don't we see where we stand?"

Una nodded rapidly. "Of course!"

Zipper grinned, "The race is probably over, but we can still rub our escape in Mal's face."

"Yeah!" cheered Joren, pumping a fist in the air.

"Pilot," I asked the speaker, "Are we ready for a jump?"

"Yes, Captain. All systems are green, or at least, the important ones are. Let's get out of here."

"Yup," I said. "Let's go."

We rushed to the cockpit, Una overtaking me and leaping into the second seat.

I paused before joining her, hesitating as I looked at the captain's chair. "Hey, Zipper?" I called. "You want it?"

"Nah, it's your ship," he said, pulling down the jump-seat behind Una. "My racing goggles are busted anyway."

I sat down, and Joren took his seat behind me. Pilot activated the thrusters, effortlessly punching through the atmosphere. The nebula whispered around us as we gained speed, rushing towards open space and the finish line beyond. Around us, the purple gasses grew thinner and thinner.

I caught a glimpse of another ship coming into view to our left as we hit clean space, and then Pilot activated the jump drive.

We jumped.

I blinked and shook my head, the pressure change setting off fireworks behind my injured nose. When my eyes refocused, I gasped.

We were in a clump of a dozen ships all making a bee-line towards the massive holographic finish line, a giant red-ribbon marking the end of the race. The ribbon was translucent, meaning that the winner had already broken through. But it was still there, meaning the race wasn't over.

We still had a chance for a number.

"YES!" yelled Joren from behind me. I could hear Zipper whooping next to him.

A large green ship suddenly flashed out of a jump right in front of us, causing me to yelp in surprise and grab my armrests. Pilot swooped nimbly to one side, swerving around the newcomer and continuing to pick up speed as he rushed us towards the finish line.

Something exploded in the engine room.

"It's fine," said Pilot. *"Don't worry about it."*

Una reached over and hit a few buttons on the dash. The announcer's feed blared across the speakers, filling the cockpit with Perk Hamlin's excited patter.

"...to* Shango's Axe, *finisher 96!* Shango's Axe *is a solo vessel captained by Shade Luper of the Titun-Abuja Colony on Mars. That means we have 20 Martian ships finishing this year, the most of any planet! This the first race where Earth hasn't taken that honor since the Jupiter Sweep of 2328. Well done, Mars! And well done, Shade!"

"...freaking Martian colonies..." muttered Una.

__"Coming up next — a battle for 97th! The fight is between the Dragonera of Earth, owned and piloted by the legendary Karlo Sainz XXVI and his sons, verses this year's entry from the Zlaka Corporation, the Metal Maiden, piloted the most recent winner of the Tour de Cymbeline, Anisa Aziz!"__

There was a burst of scattered applause and cheering from the crowd on Hub Chiba.

__"She proved to be quite the scrapper in the Tour, but can she compete with a racing dynasty?"__

We watched the main feed as *Dragonera* and *Metal Maiden* raced side by side, wing to wing, until *Dragonera* pulled ahead slightly and moved across the *Metal Maiden's* path, forcing the other ship to serve off the racing line. *Metal Maiden* corrected her course but it was too late. *Dragonera* flashed across the finish.

__"No, she can't, but a fine race for the newbie nonetheless! Congratulations to the Sainz family for their number 97 finish! It looks like we'll be hearing that name for one more generation at least! Impressive!"__

"Spicy!" said Zipper from behind me. "I had money on Sainz. At least I'll make a few buks off this fiasco."

__"We are now closing in on the end of our race, and what a race it has been! Never have we seen such bravery...or such attrition. There are only two places left — two places between immortality and obscurity. Who will be admitted into the elite ranks of the Diomedes 100? Who will be left in defeat?"__

Una typed at the controls, watching data scroll on the side screen. "He finished 3rd," she said, bitterly.

"Mal?" I asked. "He'll probably be mad about that. He wanted to win."

"If he hadn't stayed to fight you, he probably would have," said Zipper.

"Can we focus, please?" asked Joren.

We were in a pack of a dozen ships, racing neck to neck. This was anyone's race.

"Whoa!" We all jumped in surprise. A gold ship flashed out of a jump between us and the finish line, cutting off the group and taking the lead. Within seconds, the gold ship broke through the ribbon.

"What a jump! We have our 99th finisher — **Spicy Sauce!** *Captained by Rumen Yan, of the Yan Noodle Company! He is joined by his pilot, newbie Guy Cosmo. This is* **Spicy Sauce's** *third race and first Diomedes number! Congratulations, Rumen and Guy!"*

We were still in the clump of ships, gaining on our competitors with every passing second. We were the fastest, but the finish line was rushing towards us with astonishing speed. We might not have enough time...

We passed a ship painted purple to look like the nebula, then a ship with glowing blue and white stripes. There was only one ship between us and the finish line...

I looked down at the main feed, which was showing a graphic of us and the other ship.

The other ship was named the *Zenobius Zephyr*.

"Oh no!" I cried, leaning forward to grip the dash. "We HAVE to beat that ship!"

"Aye aye, Captain!" crowed Pilot.

We moved alongside them.

I looked over. The *Zenobius Zepher* was right next to us. I could see the pilot in the cockpit, a young man. We exchanged a look. Time seemed to slow as we moved slightly ahead, pushing forward, the ribbon rushing towards us.

Erebus crossed the finish line.

The ribbon burst into mile-high holographic fireworks, flashing blindingly across the sky, singling the end of the race.

We had done it.

We were the Diomedes 100.

I looked down at the dash, still not fully processing what had happened. We were on the main feed. I could see the outside of the *Erebus*, tiny worker drones flying quickly out of frame, leaving behind the number "100" in bold, glittery, prismatic white on the side of the red ship, throwing rainbows of light in all directions.

My mouth fell open. Next to me, Una slapped herself across the face. She took a fraction of a second to recover, then looked at me and started yelling, "WE DID IT!!!!"

Behind me, I could hear Joren and Zipper hastily unbuckling their seatbelts and jumping around, whooping and punching each other in celebration.

Perk Hamlin's voice came over the loudspeakers, ***"Closing out the race is our 100th finisher, the* Erebus*, captained by Cassy! She hails from Aavikko, Res4, if you can believe that! Give me some of the sand she is eating! Her crew consists of her engineer, Joren, her strategist, Una Sjöberg, and her Pilot...Pilot. They are racing in honor of the late Tef Baharia. Congratulations, Erebus!"***

Over the speakers, we could hear the crowd on Hub Chiba erupt. A chant started.

What were they saying? It was hard to tell.

"3-Out! 3-Out! 3-Out! 3-Out!"

"Hear that, folks? She may be number 100 in the race but she's number 1 in the hearts of the crowd! Everyone loves a local! And with Zipper Fanshee's disappearance and reported crash, this makes Cassy the only finisher to represent Sector 3!"

"Hey Pilot," said Zipper, "Can you let them know I'm okay?"

There was a pause as Pilot relayed the message, then Perk gasped audibly. ***"Let me get that straight — am I hearing this correctly? Zipper Fanshee is aboard the* Erebus*? Let me repeat, Zipper Fanshee is alive and aboard the* Erebus*!"***

The roar of the crowd almost blew out the speakers. *"ZIPPER! ZIPPER! ZIPPER!"*

Zipper looked sheepish, "Oh, that's my fan club. It's a little embarrassing."

I laughed. "Enjoy your fans. They must have been very scared for you."

"Yeah," said Zipper, a rueful smile twisting his lips. "Sometimes, I think they actually care about me. I'll veb-time them in a minute.

"Yeah," I replied, grinning proudly as I looked around the cockpit, the ecstatic faces of my crew beaming back at me. "Right now, let's soak this in."

"I wish we had champagne," said Una. "I always imagined popping champagne."

"I saw some energy drinks in the kitchen," volunteered Joren.

"Thanks," said Una, "but I'll pass."

We were in the lounge celebrating our incredibly unlikely finish. Zipper had urged me to capitalize on the hype and take a few interviews, but I wanted to spend this time with my friends. Pilot eventually muted the communications systems so he didn't have to bother fielding hundreds of calls. Most of them were for Zipper anyway.

It was going to take us a while to get back to Hub Chiba on standard speed. That was to be expected — the majority of other finishers were headed back on impulse as well. Most strategies had racers finish with a jump, and even the finishers who ended with a recharged drive typically didn't want to spend the kakorine. The festivities on Chiba wouldn't be in full swing for another day or two, at least. We had time.

I looked around at my friends, smiling. This was exactly like a holo. There was even music playing.

Music?

It came again, a short, chirpy melody on a repeat.

I looked around the lounge again, confused.

"Is anyone going to get that?" asked Zipper from the doorway. He was running a comb through his hair.

I got to my feet. "What is it?"

Zipper pocketed the comb and cocked his head, listening. "Sounds like a quantum transmitter. Do you have a quantum transmitter?"

"Yeah," I said, even more confused. "It's in the wreckage of *Erebus A*."

Joren turned to me. "Who has the other side?"

I gave him a look. "Mae."

Joren's face broke into a smile. "Mae! I bet she's watching the race and wants to say hi!"

"Ah, a fan call," said Zipper. "That's to be expected."

We both started for the cargo room, the other two right behind us.

Zipper was right; it was the quantum receiver. It was ringing and softly vibrating, the indicator light flashing green.

I walked over to where it rested on the floor and hit the 'talk' button. "Hello?" I said, "Mae? Is that you?"

"Hello Cassy," came Mae's voice, unnaturally calm and flat. Was still mad at me?

Mae continued, a tremor now noticeable in her tone, "There is someone here who wants to talk to you."

Drak?

"Come here, right now," a familiar male voice said.

Not Drak.

Mal.

"I went to where I left you, but you had crawled away," he continued with an audible sneer. "If I have to wait, I will start shooting. Bring my things. All of them."

Mae gave a gasp of pain and the connection went dead.

We all stared at each other.

"Ummm...what was that?" asked Zipper. "Was that Mal?"

"Yeah..." I said, slowly. "That was Mal. He's...he's on Aavikko."

"No way," Joren argued in disbelief. "How? Why?"

"It's been more than 24 hours since he jumped to the finish line," said Una, her eyes wide. "He would've gone back to our crash site at impulse speed, but once he realized we weren't there, he could have jumped straight to Aavikko."

Joren looked at me, "You told him about Mae?"

"I may have mentioned her," I said, my heart sinking. "Can we get there fast without jumping? I don't see how. Call back and tell him it will be a while. He's not thinking straight."

"Pilot?" Una asked, a question in her voice.

"Mal is a sadist," said Zipper. "He knows exactly what he's asking."

Joren's green eyes were wild, "We have to do something about Mae! She's not supposed to be involved with this!"

"Excuse me," interrupted Pilot. *"It's not entirely correct that we* **can't** *jump again. Una and I have been studying jump drive theory, and I believe I can force a second jump with the remainder of our ore. It may not work, in which case we will probably explode, and if it does work, the jump mechanism will almost certainly be destroyed. Still, it may get us to Aavikko."*

Joren nodded his head. "Great! Do it! Go!"

"Wait a second," I said, holding up a hand. "I'm fine with destroying the jump drive, but what about the rest of the engine?"

"Assuming we don't explode, the rest of the engine should remain operational."

"Pilot...what about you?"

There was a long pause.

"I...I'm not sure."

"It's pretty risky," said Una. "As much as I want to experiment, I don't want to break Pilot. After all, Mal's *probably* not going to murder your friend. I say we call his bluff and head back to Chiba."

Joren shot her a furious look, "You *do* remember that he threw Cassy out an airlock, right?"

"Pilot?" I asked. "How crazy is this, exactly?"

*"The maneuver has never been executed, only theorized. That said, I did manage a perfect jump-pause. I **am** the best Pilot in the galaxy."*

I saw Zipper straighten up and glare at the speaker, but he didn't argue.

"Does that mean you want to try it?" I asked.

"Yes."

"Then let's go. Hold on, everybody."

The jump felt normal at first. I felt the same change of pressure as the floor hopped beneath me, then fell still. I was about to congratulate Pilot when we rocked violently, explosions sounding from the engine room. A moment later there was an impact that would have thrown me across the room if I wasn't already holding on. A burning smell filled the lounge, followed by the faint sound of something spraying next door.

"Pilot!" I yelled. "Pilot, are you okay?"

There was silence.

"Pilot...?"

I looked over at Una. Her face was bloodless.

The spraying sound stopped and the smoke started to clear. The engine room's fire suppression system had worked. But there was still no sound from the speaker.

"Please, Pilot. Say something."

There was another pause, then a faint crackle.

"Something."

"Pilot!" I exclaimed, holding my chest. "Oh thank goodness! Are you okay?"

"I believe so, Captain. That just...hurt. I'm not sure how else to describe it. I...hurt. But I can be repaired. The jump drive is broken, irreparably so. I think it melted. I recommend you all get tested for radiation poisoning.

"We'll worry about that later," I said. "Let's get this over with."

We all got to our feet and headed to the exit.

"Bring your gun," I told Joren as we passed the turn to his bunk.

He looked sheepish, "Um, okay, but I'm out of ammo."

"What?"

"I used all the bullets I had on Perseyai, and I haven't bought any more. I don't like guns."

"Great," I said, sarcastically.

"Actually," said Joren, "I'm going leave the gun behind. I don't want to escalate the situation."

"Fine!" I stepped into the airlock. "Hey Pilot? Take care of the *Erebus*. If they try anything, get out of here."

"The ship has no remaining kakorine. There is no escape. I don't think you fully understand the feat I just achieved. I forced photons to behave unnaturally. Captain — does that make me a god?"

"Oh, for heaven's sake!"

"Point being, if they try to capture me, I will destroy the ship."

"Understood. Let's hope it doesn't come to that, okay?"

"Agreed."

"Wait," said Una as we were about to exit. "Shouldn't we have a plan?"

"If you have any ideas, I'm listening."

Una shook her head, her face deathly pale. "I don't know. Maybe we can talk to him. This is crazy."

"So, just to clarify, our plan is to *talk* to him?" asked Zipper as he patted a stray hair back into his pompadour.

"Do you have a better plan?" I asked.

"Nope," said Zipper, cheerfully. "Just making sure we're on the same page."

We exited the *Erebus*.

Mal was about 200 yards away, halfway in between our ship and the rusty entrance of the Res4 enclosure. His black racing ship with both a #1 and a #3 painted on the side sat on a small hill to one side, about 50 meters away. Far above us, like a distant vulture, hung the *Chaos*. Mae was being held in front of Mal like a shield, a pistol pushed to her temple. He glared at us as we approached, but occasionally he would toss a glance over his shoulder at the ramshackle gate where a handful of off-duty miners were gathered, whispering and eyeing him. I saw Drak in the crowd, his ruddy face tense.

But the main thing I noticed was that Mal was alone.

Where was his crew?

That's weird...

I didn't have much time to think about it. We were now close enough to talk. I met Mae's terrified blue eyes and gave her what I hoped was a reassuring smile.

She didn't look very reassured.

"Don't you think this is a bit much?" I said to Mal. "Let her go."

He sneered at me. "It wasn't hard finding the 'May' person you mentioned. I thought she might have a way to reach you. And I was right." He pressed the muzzle of the pistol hard against her temple, causing Mae to wince. "We are going to end this now. It can go one of two ways: One, you uninstall the AI and give it to me, and we both fly away and forget we ever met. Two, I kill a lot of people, including you *and* her," he gave Mae a shake, "and I take the AI anyway. Decide now."

Mae started to cry. My stomach twisted. Before I could think of what to do, Una stepped forward.

"You aren't getting the AI, Father."

Mal did a double-take, his eyes bulging. "Una?!" He stared at her hair, his look of surprise morphing into one of disgust. "What the hell are you supposed to be?"

"Hey!" I snapped at him. "Don't talk to her like that!"

He turned back to me. "Don't tell me how to talk to my daughter! Who are you, anyway? You are nobody. A thief and a kidnapper."

Una took another step forward. "You want to talk about kidnapping? Really?"

Mal turned his pale eyes on her, face blank, "What are you talking about?"

Una exploded, "You kidnapped me from MOM'S FUNERAL, YOU MONSTER!! You can't just do that! You can't show up one day and decide to be a dad. I'm not a doll to dress up and play with when you feel like it, then put back in the toybox." Tears welled in her large eyes.

Anger and confusion warred across Mal's face. "What are you talking about? I went out of my way to find you. I was going to give you everything!"

"You were going to give me exactly what you wanted to give me, exactly when you wanted to give it to me!"

Mal made a dismissive *pfffftt* sound. "You sound like your mother."

"Good!" yelled Una.

"You want to know about your mother?" hissed Mal. "The truth? She *never* supported my dreams of the Diomedes. That's why it ended between us. She couldn't be the partner a champion needs. But *you* understand, Una. Once I heard you loved the Diomedes, just like me, I knew I could start a legacy. *We* could start a legacy.

Una threw up her hands, "You never listened to me! You never included me! Cassy did!"

"What?" Mal looked baffled. "I listened to you! I listened to your plan! That's how I knew about Dionto's Rings!

"You stole my plan! And tried to kill me!" Una shouted.

"You weren't supposed to be on the ship!" Mal shouted back. "*She* said you weren't onboard!" He pointed at me.

I held up my hands, "Keep me out of this."

He turned to me. "I'll get to *you* in a minute, pirate."

"I'm not a pirate."

"Really? Because if it walks like a pirate, talks like a pirate—"

"I don't talk like a pirate."

"Everyone from Aavikko talks like a pirate."

"Hey!" said Una, waving her arms, "You were talking to ME, remember?"

"Yes," said Mal, turning back to her. "I was. Get on the ship. Kven will take care of you. I'm going to get my things from Cassy here, then we'll talk."

I took a cautious step forward, hands still raised. "That's never going to happen. You aren't getting the *Erebus* back. And you aren't getting Pilot. You killed him once, but he's fully in control of the ship now. He'll blow it to pieces before you take him."

"He?" Mal looked confused, "He who? The AI? What are you talking about?"

I lowered my hands. "Yes, the AI. His name is Pilot. But you know him better as Tef. Tef put his mind into Pilot before you murdered him."

"What?" Mal stared at me. "The AI is mapped to Tef? And you gave him the power to destroy himself? Do you realize that Tef was a depressive asshole with a silverleaf addiction? I can't imagine a worse personality. I'll have to reprogram that thing completely."

Una and Joren were also gaping at me.

"Whoa," said Joren. "Pilot's like, a real person?"

"No," said Mal. "It's a computer program. An incredibly advanced computer program that is MY property. Now, I want you two," he gestured at me and Joren with the muzzle of the gun, "to go join your friends behind that gate. I'm getting my AI, and once I have it, I'll release her." He gave Mae's shoulder a squeeze. "Got it? Una, go to my ship. Now!"

I shook my head at him. "You're not understanding. *You aren't getting Pilot*. Ever. Which means you have nothing to give to the Oberion League."

Mal looked at me in surprise.

"Yeah, that's right," I said. "We figured out your little secret. And I don't think you've won enough with your finish to scratch the surface of your debt with them."

Joren broke in, "I don't think your finish matters at all, not to anyone but you. They don't want your money. They want Pilot. They want to chart the nebula."

"How could you?" asked Una. "Is it true? You were going to sell out the lives of thousands of innocent children? For what? The Diomedes is just a race. It's the best race in the universe, but it's just a race."

Mal looked confused. "What do you care about the war? It has nothing to do with us. Those rebels aren't my kids. YOU are my kid, and you are a pain in the ass. Now get on my ship!"

"NO!" cried Una.

"Hi," said Zipper, interrupting with a wave. "Zipper here. I feel like you're overlooking the big celebrity in this standoff. There may not be law enforcement out here, but I have a lot of very, very loyal fans. And they are headquartered on Chiba."

"I know who you are. Do you really think I'm scared of a fan club?" asked Mal, dismissively.

"It's run by Baron Nemo Nobu. You know, Chiba's Head of Security."

The remaining traces of blood drained from Mal's face.

Zipper studied his nails with mock disinterest. "If you shoot me, you'll never be allowed on Chiba again. Just a thought."

"I think you need to get a lot further away than Chiba," said Una. "You need to run as far as you can. Just leave with what you have. Please, Dad."

Mal swung his gun at her, then seemed to realize what he was doing and pointed it back at me. His fingers dug tightly into Mae's shoulder and she yelped in pain.

Joren took a step forward, "What's your plan here? Are you going to shoot all of Res4? How much ammo do you have?" He gestured to the entrance. A dozen men and women were standing outside the gate, holding chair legs and crowbars and other improvised weapons. Their dirty faces were hard and determined. My people were ready to fight.

"You'll have to kill us all," said Joren.

Mal shook his head as if trying to clear cobwebs, then turned to Una. "Get in the racer or the killing begins, starting with your girlfriend." He steadied the gun at me. "I'm not unreasonable. I don't *want* to kill all of them, just her."

Una stepped in front of me, arms outstretched. "No, Dad. It's over."

"MOVE!" he ordered.

She didn't move. "It's over," she said again.

We all stared at each other.

Mal opened his mouth, but before a word could escape, the sound of an engine made us look around.

It was coming from Mal's racing ship.

Blasting red sand, it rose slowly into the air.

For a long moment, we watched the racer go in silence. We stood, faces upturned, staring as it crossed the sky, became a speck, and was swallowed by the *Chaos*.

"Let me guess," I said, a slow grin creeping across my face, "Kven refused to come with you on this hostage mission? He stayed behind on the racer? I *thought* he was losing faith in your leadership abilities."

Zipper snickered, "I bet the crew wants to collect that Diomedes purse without you around to hog most of it."

Mal's face was as white as a bone. "No. This can't be happening."

"Yeah, it's happening," I said, grin widening. "Let me guess, your contract with the League was a personal contract, not a ship contract? Probably didn't want to share any credit? Well, now you are a liability. The League doesn't have a reason to hunt *them* down."

Mal tore his eyes from the sky and focused on me, sneering. "What about you? The League wants your AI more than it wants *me*."

"I've been thinking about that," I said, crossing my arms and tapping a finger to my chin, "and I don't think the League knows anything about us. I don't think you told them you lost the AI. That would look pretty bad, huh?"

Mal's sneer froze on his lips.

"Hey that's a good point," Joren exclaimed. "The Calabrian Raiders know, but they are paid for secrecy. If Kven has any brains at all he'll take your Falcon, get the prize money from Chiba, ghost the League, and never look back."

Chaos moved slowly out of low orbit, disappearing into the inky blackness of space.

"Hey look, he has some brains."

"No!" Mal was breathing fast and shallow, staring at the sky. "This can't be happening. They *can't* leave me!"

"May I go now?" asked Mae in a small voice.

Mal looked down in surprise, seemingly having forgotten that he was still holding her by the shoulder. There was a moment of indecision, then he opened his hand and shoved her away.

Mae stumbled forward. Joren barely caught her before she fell in the sand.

"Hey!" said Drak. He'd been slowly creeping around the edge of the gate, trying to get closer to Mae. Now he ran up even to us, putting an arm around her. She buried her head in his chest. "Look, man," he said over the top of her red curls, speaking with unexpected authority. "I don't know what your deal is, but if I'm understanding correctly, you seem to be in a spot of trouble. Now, I don't like what you've been doing, but it's Aavikko rules that anyone who wants a job can have one. As the assistant foreman, I can offer you a deal. It will be hard work, but it's honest—"

Mal spat at him.

"—wow, rude," finished Drak.

With a final look at Una, his face inscrutable, Mal turned his back on us and walked slowly into the desert.

The six of us watched as he turned into a tiny speck, then disappeared into the horizon.

"Maybe he'll bump into Crazy Ramone and his gang," said Joren optimistically.

"Maybe he won't," replied Una, coldly.

"Um, what was that?" asked Drak.

Mae peeked out from where she was huddled against his chest. She was opening her mouth to say something when she caught sight of Zipper. Her eyes widened. "Are you really Zip…Zipper Fanshee?"

"At your service," he said with an elaborate bow, his racing tunic blowing theatrically in the breeze. He winked at her.

She stared at him for a moment, then stepped back from Drak and smoothed her dusty blue overalls, cheeks pink.

"Cassy," Drak said. "You *have* to come to the mess hall! We've been watching you race. Or, at least, we were until that guy showed up. What was that about, anyway?"

I shuffled my feet. "I'll explain later. Is the company mad at me?"

He laughed, "Are you crazy? You just got a Diomedes number and told everyone you were from Res4! We anticipate a real uptick in trade. I think the Overseer wants to give you an honorary title or something."

He and Mae set off towards the mess hall, hand in hand, the four of us following cautiously. I wasn't sure this was a good idea, and looking at Joren, he was thinking the same thing. Una looked even more uncomfortable. She crossed her arms in front of her and moved closer to me.

Drak and Mae walked into the mess hall, gesturing for us to follow. We followed.

The room exploded with cheering.

"CASSY! CASSY! CASSY! CASSY!"

I blinked in surprise.

What appeared to be the entire population of Res4 was inside, cheering, clapping, pumping their fists in the air. There were nearly a hundred people, smiling at me and chanting my name.

"Hi everyone!" I said with a wave, feeling very awkward. "Umm, look! Joren is here too!"

The crowd started chanting, "Joren! Joren! Joren!"

Miners rushed forward, shaking our hands and clapping us on the back. After a few minutes I was able to pawn them off on Joren, who seemed to enjoy the attention, and turned to Zipper.

"Hey Zipper, thanks again for everything. Do you want co-captain credit for the race? I feel like you deserve it."

He shook his head. "Thanks, but just credit me as part of the crew. What I'm more interested in is my share of the prize money. The *Tachi-Machi B* won't buy itself. My cut is 25,000 buks, correct?"

"Um," I stammered. "We have a lot of repairs to make and fuel to buy. I was planning to split the pot after we knew the costs."

Zipper paused, eyeing me, then repeated with the exact same inflection, "My cut is 25,000 buks, correct?"

I sighed. I had hoped he would take the co-captain credit and leave me more of the money.

"Yeah, sure."

"Great!" he replied with a huge smile. "That's settled. How does it feel being back home?"

I paused, unsure how to answer. "Home? I don't know about that."

He laughed, "Come on! You are a local hero!"

"That's too weird to think about," I said. "Honestly? It makes me feel like a fraud. I spent my whole life dreaming about getting out of here..." I paused, trailing off.

"But...?" Zipper prompted.

"But it's nice to see everyone so happy. Res4 never gets anything."

Zipper nodded. "I know just how you feel."

Drak walked up to us. For the first time I realized he was wearing yellow coveralls. That meant he was the assistant-foreman of sales.

"Congratulations on your promotion," I said.

He grinned. "Thanks! Things are going well, even if we are a bit short-staffed."

"I'm glad," I replied. "Oh! Since you are the assistant-foreman, you can make direct sales, right?"

He nodded.

"Well," I continued, "we need to buy some kakorine. How about 10 buks a pound?"

"10 buks a pound?" Drak laughed. "Yeah right. Try 20."

"12."

"18."

"13."

"17."

"15?"

"...15."

We pounded fists.

"Okay," I continued, "I'll need at least a ton."

"Sounds good," said Drak. "Figure out an exact amount and I'll have it loaded into your ship. You can pay me directly."

"Oh," I said, realizing a flaw in my plan. "I don't have any cash at the moment. Our prize money is waiting on Hub Chiba."

"I can give you company credit," offered Drak.

Company credit? Uh oh...

Zipper grinned at me. "I've got this. Add it to my prize money."

"Okay, that works. Thanks," I said. Then I looked over his shoulder and grinned. "By the way, I think your fan club found you."

Behind Zipper were a dozen or so miners, holding out scraps of paper for autographs and giggling.

He laughed, then turned to greet them. "Hello, friends!" he said in the bright, overly cheerful voice he used for interviews.

Mae walked up. "Hey Drak, the foreman is looking for you. Something about the shifts for tomorrow?"

Drak nodded and walked off. After watching him go, Mae turned to me. "Hi Cassy."

"Hi Mae."

There was an awkward silence.

"Thanks for leaving me the Imago 5 poster," she said after a minute. "We have it hanging in the den. You should come visit our house before you leave. It's one of the nice ones by the heap." She paused. "It really is nice."

"I'm sure it is," I replied.

Mae's eyes narrowed suddenly. "You don't have to pretend. I know you hate this place and everyone here."

"That's not true," I said quickly, blood rushing to my face. "I don't think that, I really don't. I'm sorry I made you feel that way."

Mae looked at me for a long moment, then sighed, relaxing. "I'm sorry I didn't support you either."

We looked at our feet.

"While we're apologizing," I said, "I'm also sorry for dragging you into…everything. You wanted a peaceful life and I got a gun held to your head."

"It's okay, I'm sure it wasn't your fault," she said. "You'll have to tell me the whole story. Why don't you all come over for dinner tonight? We can catch up and I'll show you the house."

"That sounds great," I said, and I meant it.

"Are you rich now?" she asked. "Having a Diomedes number and all?"

I shrugged. "Not really. Number 100 only wins us back our buy-in, which is a lot, but I'm splitting it with the crew and we have a lot of repairs to make. I'm not sure there will be much left over for me."

"Oh, okay," she said. "You want a job?"

I blinked in surprise. "What?"

"Well," she continued, "now that you and Joren are famous and Drak is an assistant-foreman, he could probably get you your jobs back. You wouldn't even have to go through training again. It's a good deal."

I stared at her. "Hell no. Are you insane?"

Mae shrugged and walked away.

A moment later Joren walked up. "How's it going? Are you and Mae okay?"

"I think so," I said. "We're all going to her place for dinner."

"That's cool," he said. "Look, Cass, I've been thinking. If you don't have any other plans, I think we should help the Free Children of Meris VI. Being back here...it's like I'm seeing it for the first time. We